A NAUTICAL TWIST

BOOK 4 BRYANT BROTHERS NOVELLA SERIES

KATHLEEN PENDOLEY

RIVERHAVEN BOOKS

E-book design by Fat Cat Design

E-book ISBN 978-1-7371403-8-2

Paperback ISBN 978-1-7371403-9-9

www.kathleenpendoley.com

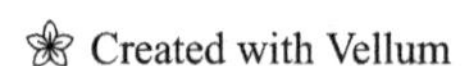

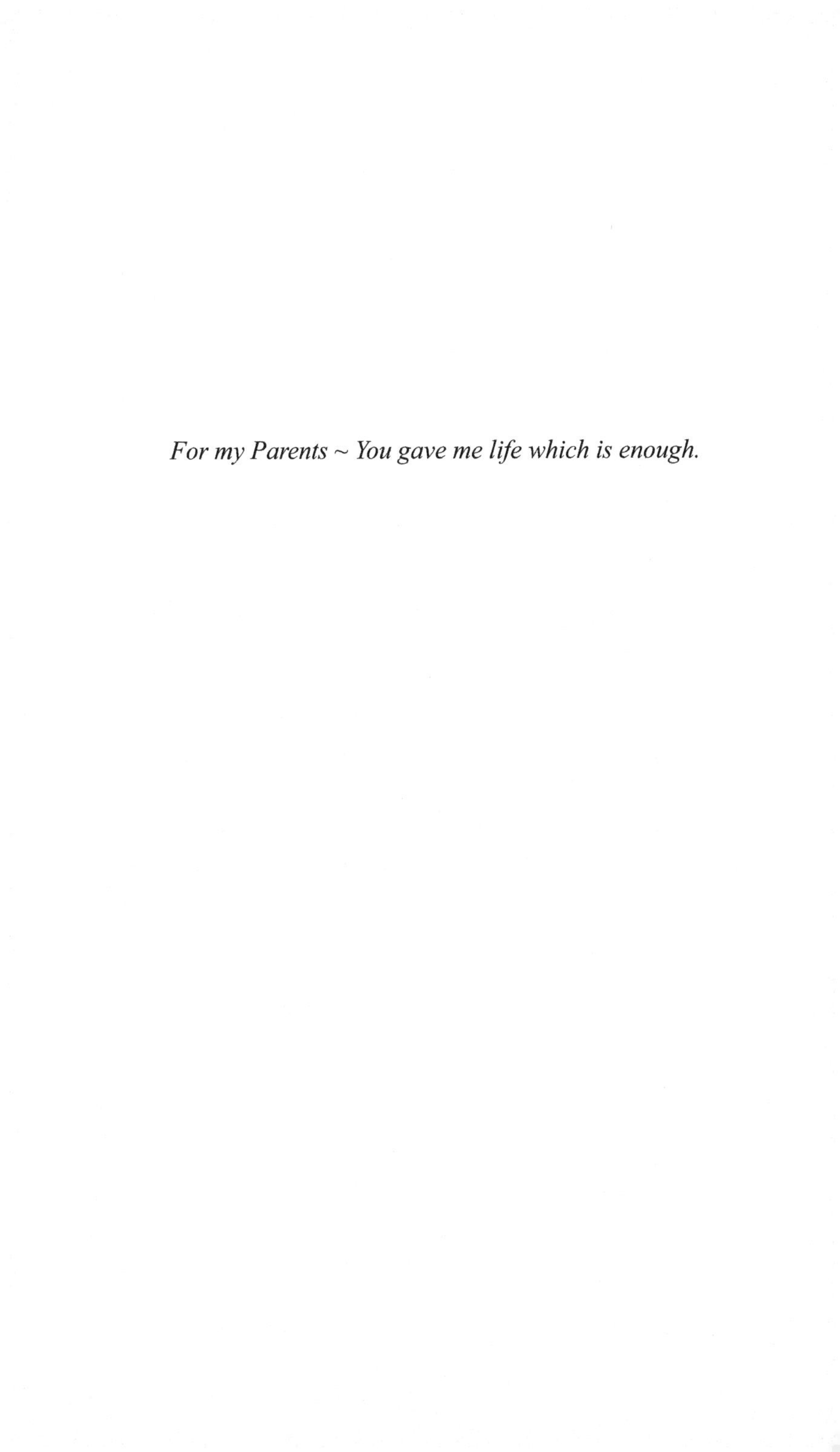

For my Parents ~ You gave me life which is enough.

1

GREG

I end up parking in a residential driveway turned paid-parking lot now that tourist season has begun. In earnest, I wind my way down a sandy, pitted path and around dozens of cars to reach the entrance of The Clam Digger Restaurant. Before pulling the door open, I grip the handle for balance and remove my shoes, emptying an enormous amount of sand. No doubt about it, I'm back in Bristlemouth Bay.

Four years in college passed in a flash, but the hard work began when I started kindergarten. My mother instilled a strong work ethic in me. The desire to discover my biological father fueled the energy I needed to get into a good program for becoming a molecular biologist. Two years to go, and my Ph.D. will be complete.

This summer, I'm continuing my internship with Uncle Jack in his private lab. I never use the formal title. He's just Jack, the man who could have been my dad if life had a more linear way of working things out.

We'll run thousands of DNA profiles together to provide

others with answers to the same burning questions I once had, like *Who am I?* and *Where did I come from?*

I was eighteen when I received the results of the DNA test. The first coincidence was that those results proved my father was Jack's brother – who was someone we'd just met by fate. Life being stranger than fiction, my mother may have created me with Mason, but her destiny was with Jack.

Today, we're celebrating Mom and Jack's third wedding anniversary at the oldest restaurant in town. I push the heavy wood door open and find the place hopping, per usual, and wonder why I bothered cleaning out my shoes. They crunch over gobs of sand and free popcorn as I make my way to the private function room.

Someone propped open the French doors dividing the function hall from the main dining area with sandbags made from lobster bibs. Because one wall is glass, I can see everyone. Where they've had an hour's head start, Mom, Jack, and all their friends and family are engrossed in conversation, drinking, and dancing, oblivious to my arrival. My mom's laugh carries louder than anyone's, and, no surprise, it's Jack who has her in stitches. The love they found endures, and I'm happy for them.

That is until I see *her* and hide like an idiot behind a thin column. Though I'm lanky at six foot three and 170 pounds, the post is four inches wide and useless for cover.

She ignores me as she balances food trays over her shoulders, one in each hand, heavy with finger foods. Shrimp cocktail and fresh-baked crab cakes piled high on top of one, oysters on the half-shell fill the other. Is there any nastier fare on the planet than the phlegmy feel of a living creature sliding down your throat?

My stomach rumbles, but I'll have to wait until she clears

the area. It's the same thing every summer I return between semesters—keeping one eye out at all times to avoid my ex-girlfriend, Lia. It makes work on my dissertation seem relaxing and straightforward, and my desire to be back at school *right now* powerful.

Still, I can't help watching her every move. Similar and different, she's as pretty as the day we met four summers ago.

Bonfires are a big deal on the island, and the first night my mom and I arrived on vacation, I was invited. Typically, only the locals attended the pre-summer season parties, but Brandon, the first townie I met, said it would be okay for me to go. I guess he wanted to show me some appreciation since I helped him change the inner tube on his bicycle tire after a rusty nail had flattened it.

That night, Lia glowed brighter than the twelve-foot inferno backlighting her. Her day spent at the beach segued into an evening with close friends, and the pale blue bikini she wore under a transparent white beach cover-up did nothing to hide the gifts nature had bestowed. I fell hard and found myself by her side, my feet moving of their own accord.

She was as smart, sweet, and friendly as she was pretty, sealing the deal of my interest. We talked late into the night about her life on the island and mine in Providence, Rhode Island.

Lia told me how she would inherit The Clam Digger Restaurant from her father, who had inherited it from his father. Her upbringing was vastly different from mine, having both parents present and engaged. Going to college and getting a degree was never a dream for her as she was born and raised within the walls of the business and planned to die there as well.

I explained my goal of becoming a scientist and touched briefly on how finding my dad was the catalyst. If I hadn't wanted to study genetics for so long, being a police detective might have been a possibility—solving riddles and puzzles are mental gymnastics my brain loves to play.

We started dating that night and spent most of our time running on the beach, kissing under the dock, and snagging free meals in the restaurant's kitchen. We never ran out of things to talk about or ways to make each other laugh. Any night there was a party on the beach, we'd be there together. Before long, we'd move from the group and get lost in conversation again.

If only we could have that period back! Even if it didn't seem so at the time, life was simpler that season. Being eighteen and not knowing your paternity can be painful, and the discovery overwhelms you. Through both experiences, there was Lia, and I tossed her away, foolishly and cowardly, in one moment of teen uncertainty.

"Hey! Greg Madison is in town."

A familiar voice calls my name, clapping me on the back from behind and making me jump. I turn and exchange a fist bump with my friend.

"I thought that was you. What're you doing skulking around? Your mom and Jack have been looking for you since they arrived."

"Hey, Brandon. Nice hat." His natty baseball cap reads, "Feelin' Beachy."

"I got it from your mother."

"Seriously? Is that a Yo' Momma joke?"

His upper lip snarls, and he recoils. "Shit, no! Your mother just gave it to me, for graduation. You're not the only hotshot around here." Brandon winks then shakes my hand. Congratulations on the 4.0."

"Thanks. You too. Guess I better say hi to the fam and then I'll get to dig in to the delicious fare you created." My hunger cranks, knowing it's Brandon running the kitchen tonight.

Our family, like many, is convoluted. Brandon is my Uncle Gabe's fiancee's son, so sort of my step-cousin. He also used to work for my Uncle Dan's wife, Clara, a professional baker. Both men are Jack and my father's brothers. So, Brandon and I are related but not related. Get it? No? No one does.

I watch Lia exit the banquet space with the empty trays held under one arm. She swipes her wrist across her forehead sprinkled with perspiration as she passes by swiftly.

"Ahh," Brandon says, following her with his eyes, same as me. "I almost forgot you two were an item. Too bad you screwed that up. She's a fun gal."

"Yeah. I better get inside."

Brandon's good-natured laugh bristles. I'm not going to ask what he meant by "fun gal." He gets to work close to Lia almost every day. It doesn't take a molecular geneticist to figure it out—especially not one who already knows the answer.

"See ya!" Brandon waves and heads back to the kitchen.

I'm unfamiliar with the two waitresses who follow me in to the party; their trays weighed down with boiled lobsters, fried clams, tons of sides—French fries, coleslaw, and the like. I lighten their load by grabbing two plates for myself.

My mom rushes me, getting the attention of everyone in the room, calling, "Greg! My baby's home!" and kisses me on the cheek before Jack hands her a meal. Balancing his dish in one hand, he half-hugs me with his free arm. "Great to have you back, Kiddo."

"It's good to be back," I tell him, surprising myself when

I realize it's true. In the back of my mind I tell myself, *I'm not here to find a girlfriend or revisit the past. I'm here for a made-to-order internship.* Reuniting with my dad, who passed away shortly after I was born, wasn't a possibility. Not to mention that my mom couldn't have picked him out of a line-up. So even though that dream could never be realized, I scored to discover this whole crazy family. And having my uncle-slash-stepdad a geneticist was the icing on one of Aunt Clara's cakes. Over the past few years, Jack's lab practically became my second home, and working with him is both educational and rewarding.

"Did you say 'hello' to your uncles yet?" My mother has always been a stickler for manners. If I hadn't been about to turn eighteen when we met Jack, she'd have me calling him Mr. Bryant to this day.

"I just got here." I dunk a handful of fried onion rings in ketchup, and she knocks them out of my hand before they reach my mouth.

"Do it before you eat. They've missed you terribly."

Jack's no help when I turn to him, mouth hanging, hands held up, beseechingly.

"Sorry, Greg. I'm legally obligated to back my wife up in all situations. So, young man, you'd better put that fork down, or I'll—" He cuts himself off, laughing at how inept he is at this being a lousy step-dad ploy.

Still, I'd like to know how he would finish the sentence. "What? Or you'll what?" I chide, standing a little more on my toes and peering down at his puny five-eleven frame.

With my mom standing between us, Jack is bold enough to answer. "I'll ground you! That's right. You'll have to wipe down the counters and clean up the used slides, and I won't let you run any DNA tests for two weeks."

"Meany."

We all laugh.

"Okay, well I'm hungry so I am going to finish the obligatory meet and greet before my food cools. I'll leave with my pride intact at having the last word. Don't eat my onion rings!"

"Colleen, did you raise him this way?" Jack asks my mom.

"He must get it from your side of the family."

Jack laughs, and I just walk away, shaking my head.

Uncle Dan, the oldest Bryant brother, sits next to his wife, Clara. They eat similar meals: lobster, baked potato, seaweed salad, and fresh-baked rolls. Meanwhile, the man sitting at Dan's left side, Uncle Gabe, shoves his potato and a fluffy buttered biscuit onto Alicia's plate, his face a mask of pain since he hates carbs and junk food. Though I've noticed he'll make exceptions for Aunt Clara's confections, so he's probably making room.

At least, I hope she made dessert. Just seeing Clara has me craving cakes, pies, and cookies, even though, similar to Gabe, I try to maintain a clean diet and exercise regimen.

Dan has a dad-bod on the other end of the spectrum, but no kids to excuse it. He doesn't care. Keeping Clara happy and making sure every animal on the island is healthy at his small veterinary clinic are his priorities. A little *extra Dan*, as he claims, never hurt anyone.

I shake the men's hands and kiss the ladies on the cheeks.

As different as can be, Clara, Alicia, and my mom have become best friends. It's not just an expectation to get along since they are legally related (or, in Alicia's case, almost so) —they genuinely like each other too.

"Hey, Alicia! Nice to see you." I lean down to give her a peck on the cheek, and while she's distracted I grab her extra biscuit with my free hand. Standing up straight, I say, "Let me help you out by getting rid of this for you." Swallowing it in two bites, I become well aware that Brandon hasn't forgotten anything Clara taught him. The bread melts in my mouth, and I can't resist snagging Uncle Dan's portion before he can drop his fork.

"Hcy! I was going to cat that!" Dan pulls his platc back and protects it with his forearm.

"Let him have it, Dan," Clara admonishes. "He's a growing boy, and you already ate two."

"He's a man, and you need to stop mollycoddling him, woman!"

Clara hands me her bread with a perfectly manicured hand and pushes the rest of her fried clams my way.

"You're my favorite aunty," I tell her between bites.

"Hey!" Alicia nails the back of my hand with her fork hard enough to leave tiny red divots in the skin. "You told me I was when you were up for Christmas break."

"That's cuz I thought bozo here was going to marry you. Until then, you're not technically my aunt."

"That's Uncle Bozo to you," Gabe mutters, admonishing me with butter smeared on his mouth like lipstick from the corn on the cob, threatening to dribble down his chin. He looks like a little kid with the stupid bib tied tight around his neck. "And I'd marry her in a second." His thumb hitches toward Alicia. "She's the hold-out."

"Why buy the cow?" she teases. Why they remain engaged and never plan a date is their secret. The rest of the family suspects it's how they keep the relationship feeling exciting and new.

"Clean yourself up, Uncle Bozo." I toss him a napkin, wiping my own greasy hands on my shorts. "Mom said I had to say hello to all of you before I could eat, and I'm starving, so hello and goodbye."

"We love you!" four of my favorite people call from behind me.

"Love you more!" I tell them over my shoulder. They beam like fools until I add, "Old folks are so easy to please."

Together, they grab biscuits from a second basket and pummel my retreating back with soft bullets of bread.

2

LIA

Banquet shifts are the worst, particularly when you're trying to avoid every person in attendance. Living on this tiny spit of land has trained me to wear blinders at all times, but tonight they're being tested to a breaking point.

It's bad enough I've had to walk by Greg six times already. I had to talk to his mom, Colleen, about the order, reassuring her we wouldn't run out. She's polite and discreet, but I detect a hint of judgment in her crystal blue eyes whenever she looks at me, reducing me to a child-like state.

Biting the inside of my cheek, not to spew apologies in her face, I bolt past her when she's distracted as I make my way back to the kitchen to switch my empty tray for one brimming with seafood. Part of me wants her to bring up the embarrassing moment we shared years ago so we can hash it out, but what would be the point? The past is over, the future before me, and tonight I will have the big talk with my dad.

I swallow down my nervousness and focus on bussing trays.

The kitchen is an inferno, with all the tables filled to the max and a line of take-out orders never letting up at the reception desk.

I tap Mary, a waitress new to The Clam Digger this year, on the shoulder and ask, "Can we switch? You can keep all the tips if you finish up with the party, and I'll take care of your section."

Mary tends to be crabby and impatient with the staff but friendly and conciliatory with patrons, so she makes a ton in tips.

Tonight, money means nothing to me: pride and shame reign.

She quirks an eyebrow but doesn't question my motives. It's a better deal for her by a mile.

"You got it."

After Mary gives me the rundown of her area, I text the hostess about the change, and Mary and I start filling up our trays accordingly.

It's always busy during tourist season, and the weekends keep us hopping. If we didn't shut down almost half the year with the seasonal lull and irregular weather patterns, we'd be rolling in money. But, same as his dad, my father, Sam, has busted his butt to keep the business marginally in the black. It's what I plan to talk to him about tonight. I have ideas he may or may not like, but since the business will soon be mine, he has no choice but to listen.

I ease open the right-hand swinging door of the kitchen, checking to be sure Colleen, Jack, and especially Greg are nowhere around, before exiting and heading outside to feed clientele dining on the dock. It's oddly a relief and a let-down knowing I won't see the trio for the rest of the night.

"What do you mean you're giving it to Steve Miller? What the hell does he know about restaurants? He's an artist." I put the word in quotes. Steve makes souvenir frogs, turtles, and snakes, using seashells that wash up on shore and massive googly eyes from the craft store. You can't say the company's name without a droll expression and a shake of the head, which I do now just thinking about it. Stevie Sells Seashells. The dumbest moniker of all time and the ugliest creatures you've ever laid human eyes on.

Getting back to the subject at hand, with my fists on my hips, I ask, "And how is he related? You always say, 'A Jeffries started the Clam Digger, and it will end with a Jeffries.'"

Making a "Kuh" sound, I rest my case.

This conversation has not gone according to plan. I saw us having a bonding father-daughter moment, planning this beautiful future where Sam flies off to Florida with my mom to live with every other retiree in the country, and I make the business flourish.

Steve comes over to our house for dinner one Sunday a month. He has for years, ever since his parents moved to Florida, because he was "lonely" and lived next door. Kind of a dork, Steve only gets along with those a generation or more older than him. I'm a generation younger, and he's never been more than background noise to me, like the Mozart my parents play on the record player during those Sundays he joins us for roast beef—or any fare that isn't seafood-related.

The charts and graphs, which back up my claims on how I would manage the restaurant differently, wrinkle in the stranglehold of my fists. The red ink stains my palms like blood, and I'd like to smear it on somebody's face. Steve's would be best, but I'm sure he's home, fast asleep hours into sticking to his seven o'clock bedtime as the old folks do. It is Saturday night after all.

"Princess, be reasonable." Dad leads me past the desk to the tattered leather couch in the corner, used mainly to stack paperwork. Old receipt books, computer printouts, and expired flyers from the front window, advertising everything from goods and services to missing pets, fall to the floor as we squeeze within.

"You don't want this headache. Your mother and I want you to be happy, and chasing every last penny and buck won't get you there. Find yourself a nice guy with a good head on his shoulders as your mother did." He elbows me in the side, waggling his bushy gray eyebrows. "You're a pretty girl, but looks don't last forever." Clucking his tongue while snapping his fingers, he gets more ludicrous with his final utterance, "Get in on the ground floor, so to speak."

Who is this guy? My parents raised me in the restaurant. Saltwater runs through my veins, melted butter lines my arteries, and sand must fill the empty spaces within, for it's here, suspended on a dock over the ocean, where I'm grounded and home.

As a little girl, left mainly to my own devices while grown-ups ran around me, cooking, serving, and dropping off supplies, I made up games to play. My first memory is making friends with lobsters, lining them up like unwilling soldiers on the kitchen floor as they awaited their doom in the massive boiling pots above them on the stove.

Our black cat, Mr. Twinkles, would overreact when rounding the corner, every time the first time. Instead of finding a bowl of kibbles, he'd stumble on the unearthly beings and leap four feet in the air, back arched, fur fluffed out, doubling his size. I'd laugh like crazy until one of the chefs would lead me from the kitchen to the hostess stand to color in placemats and play with a basket filled with hairless, naked Barbie dolls. I'd wrap them toga-style in napkins and color their heads with a black magic marker.

Trying not to rage at my father and lose more ground with my plans, I focus on my words and elucidate slowly. "What's with the sexism all of a sudden, Dad? I'm calling red-herring. You've always let me play with all kinds of toys, associate with anyone who came through these doors, and join any sports team. I won as many awards in soccer as ice skating. You taught me how to swing a hammer and use a drill, and Mom showed me how to put a full set of fake nails on in fifteen minutes or less. I'd say I'm pretty well-rounded for a restaurant rat."

My dad rests his arms on his thighs and pinches the bridge of his nose. The truth should be a doozy.

I tuck my hands under my knees and brace myself.

"Do you remember when you were in high school and things got tight financially? You were the only student in your grade who couldn't go on the trip to Washington."

"I remember. The hurricane wiped everything out the year before. The rebuild went over schedule, and we had to run things from a food truck."

Talk about food lines—one night, I counted a hundred bodies waiting in line. I had to walk up and down, handing out free samples and small water bottles to keep the throngs happy and hydrated.

"Well, we were already strapped. Nana and Papa survived so long in the nursing home that our meager savings and the assets in their estate dried up. We had to take out a loan to get them cremated. Then we spent our last dime on the road trip we all took to Niagara Falls to get your mind off the D.C. trip."

"Oh, so I ruined everyone's lives because I was upset the

whole town would know we were broke?" Back then, it was bad enough that I had the oldest parents in my class, but telling him now seems petty.

"No, Princess. We also went to spread your grandparents' ashes. We didn't want to make you any more upset, so we poured them into a cardboard box, packed them in the trunk of the car, and left the urns on the mantle."

Shocked at the admission, I whisper, "I talk to them every day." It's part of my routine, telling them "goodbye" before I leave and "hello" when I return. It's not uncommon for me to say goodnight on my way up to bed or tell them my problems. "I've been connecting to a vase?"

His sorry perfunctory, Dad returns to the uncomfortable tale. "You wouldn't come sightseeing with us that first day, so we crossed into Canada and found a quiet, dead-end street with an open field and tossed them into the wind.

"They spoke wistfully about going to the Falls for their honeymoon and always wanted to go back. They never did while they were alive, so we offered them the next best thing."

"Okay, so what does any of that have to do with the restaurant?"

The ancient cuckoo clock strikes midnight, the whimsical chime contrasting with the heavy atmosphere.

"Steve's parents loaned us the money to finish some of the more costly repairs, the sinking of new pilings being the biggest. Cranes aren't cheap, you know. And we needed it here for almost a month."

"Islanders have historically helped rebuild after every storm. You told me the first time was only two years after the original was built in 1946, right after World War II. Isn't that what islanders do? Help each other out?"

"Well, most. And the Miller's did, to the tune of fifty

thousand dollars. Because of the extraordinary amount, I made a gentleman's agreement with George and Rhonda. The deal was, if we weren't able to pay them back with interest by mid-August this year, they would own the restaurant."

"What's a gentleman's agreement?" I ask, lost.

"We shook on it."

The silence lingers until I burst out laughing. "You shook hands with the guy, and now I lose my heritage? No, Dad. Sorry. You can apologize, tell him you renege, lose a bit of pride or integrity, whatever it takes, but I'm getting this restaurant." I smooth the wrinkles out of my documents as best I can. "Read through my ideas. This place will be turning a major profit in five years or less." I stick them under his nose, rattling them. "Look!"

He pushes them away, standing up to pace the carpeted floor. "We have an agreement in writing. The lawyer made it official a month ago. Without a miracle, and I'm talking bringing in five times what we normally do to cover the principal portion of the loan, The Clam Digger transfer's to Steve's name at midnight on August twentieth."

"Dad, please listen to reason and hear me out. Ask them for an extension. These are great ideas. Weddings, after-prom parties, even the gathering after a funeral. I've included every reason people get together for food. I've changed parts of the menu, found new vendors who don't charge as much, and included the potential for expansion. All I need is a little time."

It looks like I'm sunk when he sighs and his shoulders slump. Every day of his sixty-five years hangs from his tired frame, and I hate causing him pain. But I also hate the thought of this place in the hands of mister zero personality or potential.

"Dad, listen. Really listen. I know you care about Steve. I

don't know why, but you do. But don't you see? We might as well close now if he's the only option. No one wants to be around him. Maybe that's his fault, or maybe the luck of the DNA draw. Even you would admit he's a—" I'm at a loss. "What word did they use in your sock-hop days? A square?"

"Hey, watch that." He smiles for the first time, and in it I find a glimmer of hope. "I was the cool guy in the disco that all the ladies wanted to dance with." He stands up, pulls me up and close, and prances around the tight space using his cool disco moves. "We would have called a guy like Steve a putz or a jive turkey."

"And that's who you want to hand over our family legacy to?"

We stop dancing in the center of the room and drop our arms.

He shakes his head. "No. But we don't have five years or even five months until it transfers into his name. More like two, which translates to impossible."

"Can't I at least try?"

"No harm trying, Princess. I think you're wasting your time, but I'll do whatever I can to help." He shrugs, tucking his hands into the pockets of his chino's.

Before he can change his mind, I beg, "Please! Read through my plan, and we'll discuss it with Mom over breakfast. Deal?"

He agrees with a nod and accepts the stack of papers.

Using his favorite 1970's slang, I say, "Catch you on the flip side!" and leave with what I came to get—mostly.

3

GREG

"Hand me that chart and hit the lights, would you?" Jack says, holding the lab door and the keys to lock it in his hands. "Mrs. D'Marco goes to sleep immediately after the six o'clock news."

He shoves the papers under one arm and secures the lock. After letting Ryder relieve his aging bladder on a nearby holly bush, we jump into Jack's new truck with me riding shotgun and Ryder on my lap.

"Do you think you'd get in trouble if the state found out you brought this guy to work?"

At ten years old, the pup's face is gray around the muzzle, but his eyes are still sharp and bright. He turns in a tight circle three times before we exit the parking lot and promptly falls asleep on my lap. Even when he's in the lab, the snug ball is his standard pose, working under our feet, chasing the incoming tide in his dreams.

"Close us right down!" Jack karate-chops the air. "And they'd be right—technically. But all Ryder does is sleep. He barely moves enough to release dander or drop fur, and the threat of contaminating a sample is lower than low."

Changing topics, he asks, "You ready to do the talking this time?"

"Do I have to?" a queasy stomach and a light sheen of sweat on my brow have me questioning my ability to relate to someone so much older with serious information, and I try to get out easy. Maybe Jack, deep down, wants to tell Mrs. D'Marco himself that her instincts were right: the man who raised her as his own was not her biological father, and she's one hundred percent English. Her mother's story about her relative coming over on the Mayflower and marrying a Cherokee warrior is a total fabrication. I've learned just how common these false family lore are after working with Jack three summers in a row.

Jack shoots me a look of concern. "If talking to a sweet, ninety-year-old woman is too much, maybe you're better suited for the medical side of genetics. Stay in a lab. You're terrific at it, and your ideas of how to streamline things show you have management potential. You could run a lab of your own someday."

"I was hoping to run yours together."

"That was the plan, but will it be enough for you? You're way smarter than me. Running DNA samples all day for the rest of your life might get monotonous faster than you think."

In less than three miles, two right-hand turns, and a single stop sign, we arrive at the nursing home. Jack visits a few times a month to fill folks in on their heritage. He's well known among the year-round residents and is loved by all the ladies over fifty. I know we'll be lucky to get out of Mrs. D'Marco's room by six, but I'm hoping we can manage so I can head up to Boston to meet Brandon at Fenway Park. Sox versus Yankees would suck to miss.

Before exiting the truck, my eyes scan the area. A nurse's aide pushes a man in a wheelchair, and three elderly women sit by the front door, protected under an awning from the hot summer sun, playing cards. The coast is clear as expected.

Since breaking it off with Lia forever ago, I've learned her habits and schedule inside and out. Creepy, no. It's for her own good as well as mine. She hates my guts, and I have no defense. What would I say if ever the unthinkable happened and I found myself alone with her? "Sorry I didn't lock the bedroom door and my mother came home unexpectedly?" I shudder involuntarily at the thought.

"Nerves making you cold?" Jack asks, holding the door so Ryder and I can enter the facility first.

"No," I reply.

Once inside the cool, well-lit interior, the smell of industrial cleaner, chicken soup, and urine replaces the outdoor scent of the ocean.

As her name tag indicates, Hazel, the volunteer receptionist, points us in the right direction after smiling coyly at Jack and asking if he was still married to my mom. She's roughly eighty-five.

"We just celebrated three years, Hazel, but you'll be the first to know if it ever gets rocky." He lets her down gently then we race to catch the elevator. The doors close as we board, saving us from witnessing her heartbreak.

The sportscaster screaming from Mrs. D'Marco's television warns us to be quick about getting down to business. It's the last segment of the news hour; she could fall asleep at any moment.

Jack knocks on the doorframe. "Hello, Mrs. D'Marco. Can we come in?"

The bedridden woman sits upright, the bedding surrounding her piled high. "Come in, Jack! I was afraid you wouldn't make it tonight. It's getting late."

Her brain is sharp and alert, but after years with diabetes, she's missing one foot and part of one leg. Her smile, though, is engaging and full of kindness and affection.

"We're sorry about that." Jack gestures to me as we take the seats. "This is my stepson, Greg. Greg, Mrs. D'Marco. Greg helps me out at the lab whenever he's on break from college."

"Hello," I mumble nervously before explaining, "Sometimes we get caught up in what we're doing, and the hours get away from us." I rap the chart on my knee. "We have it all here now. Are you ready?" The more I talk, the more confident my voice sounds.

Mrs. D'Marco nods enthusiastically, and I fill her in.

"So, we proved you were right about dad and that mom was wrong about the Native American story. And we found your family is distantly related to King James the Second."

Mrs. D'Marco is intrigued, particularly with the royal connection, and she's not upset about our findings. I discover how enjoyable this part of the job is—matching a face and rich life experience with the lab results is even more intriguing than the darkest mystery novel or well-researched detective movie.

I'm more certain than ever that this lab and this island are where I belong.

Boston doesn't smell much different than a nursing home, I realize after stepping off the Green Line near Fenway Park. All you have to add is car exhaust to the medley, and you've nailed it—urine included. So it's no surprise to witness a guy standing in the shadows of a narrow alley, adding his bodily fluids to the *mélange*.

Only a few minutes remain before the game starts to find

our seats. Brandon waits for me at the entrance. He offers to grab beers and hot dogs so I can catch the entire game. The lines are tremendously long, so it's easy to say yes.

What a place! The Green Monster in left field…Wally the Red Sox team mascot entertaining kids in the seats by first base…and the Citgo sign in Kenmore Square—it's all here. The pitcher warms up in the bullpen, players stretch on the sidelines, and the scoreboard displays the team names and zero-zero ties. It's just like on TV, only more exciting with the hordes trying to find their seats and vendors already hawking foam hands, peanuts, and popcorn.

The Red Sox are first at bat. Christian Arroyo hits the ball into the crowd over left field. A fan just caught the pitch of a lifetime, and the Sox scored their first home run.

Lucky stiff! Our seats are in a dead zone off the right-field that rarely, if ever, has a ball sail in. We're not catching anything here but a wave. The first one goes through the crowd as Brandon scoots through the masses sitting near the aisle to take his seat behind a post.

"You wanna switch?" I offer. So far, he's bought the tickets and the food. The least I can do is give him a better view.

"Naw. I'm here all the time. Half of the enjoyment is people watching, trying to guess who gets shitfaced first."

He points out the most likely candidates and my stomach drops.

Lia. She's here. It appears she's on a date with some guy in a Yankees cap.

Let your guard down for two seconds, and this is what you get. I slacked on my watch, and Bam! There she is. Why would I look for her off-island? She never leaves. Except she does with idiots with a death wish, and not because he's wearing the enemy's cap. He's groping her mercilessly, like a middle school kid in a darkened theater.

Lia pushes with all her might against his wandering hands, her knee raised to fend him off further.

Before thought factors in, I'm on my feet, yelling, "Hey! Get your hands off of her!"

The asshole turns, gives me the finger, and resumes his bad behavior. He's older than us by thirty years, the contrast between him and Lia stark.

What is she doing with an idiot like him?

Before I can reach the aisle, Brandon takes a shortcut and leaps over two empty chairs on the other side of the metal post. He rips off the guy's Yankees cap and tosses it into the crowd.

Wearing a Red Sox T-shirt, a heavily bearded man catches it and acts as if it burns, flinging it away to land in another lap. The blond lady shrieks and throws it forward another three rows. It goes on like this until it reaches the first row over the dugout. Quickly, over the wall, it lands where Wally, the mascot, picks it up and wipes his massive green butt with it to the amusement of everyone but a few Yankee fans who are smart enough to keep their booing low-key.

I'm hardly aware of any of it. Brandon is gone after taking the idiot with him by the collar. Lia and I stand alone amid thousands, staring at each other, dumbfounded.

"Greg?" She says my name as though trying to place how she knows me.

I'm trying not to grab her and kiss her until she's mine again. *She's even more beautiful up close.* The words come back, a memory. It's the same thought I had the night we gave our virginity to one another. I'd held her and touched her many times before that night, but somehow, in that single moment, when we surrendered fully to our love, she overwhelmed me with the perfection of her beauty.

Her lips pucker like she's eaten a lemon. "Oh. Right. It's you."

Even I can tell in my lust-filled state, she's not interested in a kiss down memory lane, and I take a step back, giving us both space.

My phone pings an incoming text from Brandon. He's not coming back. The police caught him "escorting" Lia's date out the gate, and now he's stuck in a room at the stadium, waiting to be questioned.

"Should I wait for you?" I text back.

He responds, "Naw. It's not my first time at bat," followed by three hysterical laughter emojis. "Enjoy the game. I'll catch up with you tomorrow."

Lia reads through her text message and then sighs. "Great! I'm stuck without a ride." She grabs her bag, tucking it underneath her arm after swilling the rest of her beer.

"You were going to leave with that assho—hat?" This female infatuation with the "bad boy" is ludicrous—and this is from a guy whose father was one.

"Ah. Not from around here," Lia tells me sarcastically as she starts climbing over bodies toward the aisle. "I have to figure out how to get home."

"Lia, wait up!"

She keeps heading for the exit.

The fans blocking us in are unprepared for the two of us coming through at once, and it's a more complicated struggle for me to climb over the many laps. After spilling someone's soda and stepping in a bag of popcorn propped on the ground, I lose sight of her while I pay an angry mother for my misstep.

I catch up to Lia before she can reach the street and grab

her by the arm, breathlessly offering, "You can come home with me."

"You drove?"

"Only to the commuter rail parking lot. But I know how to take the train."

She rolls her eyes but relents. "Fine. Just do me a favor, though."

She has no idea, but I'll do anything she asks.

"What?"

"Don't talk to me." With a finger in my face, she warns, "Not a word."

I press my lips together tightly and nod before pointing in the direction of the Kenmore Square train stop.

4

LIA

Kenmore Square has the appearance of a mosh pit without strobe lights and darkness. If Greg weren't so tall, I'd be lost already with so many bodies around us. As it is, I have to push my way through countless strangers to keep up. Finally, he reaches back, and I grab his hand to stay close.

I need to get home and put this awful day to rest.

The plan began as a bribe and ended up a public sexual assault. I decided to buy baseball tickets for Steve. (I should have known the jerk would be a Yankees fan!) He's fanatical about sports, probably because he could never play himself, with his asthma, awkwardness, and bad knees excuses. At least that was what he bragged about on the car ride up to Boston.

"Playing games is for boys, not grown men if you catch my drift," he'd said while stuck in traffic on I-93. He touched my knee, and I pushed him away, pointing out the windshield to redirect his attention.

"Look, we're moving." Then I pulled my skirt down as

low as possible and turned my legs toward the passenger door.

Just thinking about his clammy wet fingers, the creepy-crawlies return as shudders skitter up and down my spine.

The plan was I'd supply the tickets and beer, and he'd get drunk enough to agree to hand over the business to its rightful owner: me. Yes, a simple plan, but my hope was, therein, lay its genius.

Not so.

Instead of having a few relaxing beers, Steve pounded the equivalent of a six-pack by the time Brandon tore him off of me. Steve had dropped his last plastic container under the empty seat in front of him and pounced, taking me by surprise.

I couldn't see or breathe—he was on me so fast.

Brandon always has my back when we're at work. How he and Greg ended up sitting so close behind us at such a time of need feels almost too miraculous to be a coincidence. As I'm pulled around pedestrians this way and that, barely keeping up with Greg's longer stride, I say a little prayer of gratitude to whoever listens up there.

Somehow every person in the city crams into the compartment of the Green Line train, leaving no empty seats and hardly enough space to stand near a pole. Greg's longer arm grasps an overhead bar, and I'm stuck, monkey in the middle, with nothing to hold onto.

Without a word, Greg wraps one strong arm around my waist and pulls me close, allowing enough space for my messenger bag to hang down my back and prevent the atrociously stinky man behind me from cuddling up and spooning my bum a second time.

We sway side to side as the trolly races to the next stop,

gears grinding and clanging, as though Greg and I are dancing to a terrible country ballad about perverts, B.O., and bad ideas.

Standing there, I examine where Steve spilled beer on my white cotton tank top. Not only did the cheap brew ruin my shirt, the aroma now resides in my olfactory senses. But with my face inches from Greg's fresh white T-shirt, close enough to feel his heat emanate on my skin, I remember how he smelled that first summer. Bonfires, ocean, and rose petals, all suspended in Greg's natural elementary scent.

Now and then, during the four years since we've stood this close, I'll catch a whiff of something that comes close but never satisfies. Somehow, though I can't enjoy Greg's aroma right this second, the thought that it's right there, between us, leaves me feeling quenched.

By the time we're seated on the less crowded outbound commuter rail, heading for the South Shore, fear settles in my belly the same place it has lived all summer.

How am I ever going to come up with so much money when all of my ideas are rotten? I will n*ever* go near Steve or be alone with him again. Daddy-o isn't going to like what I have to tell him. Learning that Steve attacked me may not save the business, now that it involves lawyers, but it will put an end to the awkward Sunday dinners. That's something. But bargaining is out.

I've contacted the entire population of Bristlemouth Bay —about three hundred year-round residents, not counting children. I've offered everything from discounted wedding packages to evening inlet cruises manned by yours truly in a Catamaran for six. There is nothing I *won't* do to save the business, and from all the rejections I'm getting, nothing others *will* do to help.

I'm being unfair. Some have tried to throw me a line. Clara, Greg's aunt, offered to create a new dessert menu, and we could split the profits down the middle. But with Pam's Parlor so close, most of our guests prefer to prolong their summer fun and stroll down to her establishment for an ice cream cone, sundae, or frappe after filling up on our clam strips.

Of course I said yes to Clara, but it won't have time to make a difference.

A few friends from high school are getting married, but they already have halls booked, limos rented, and their happily-ever-afters nailed down.

I need something big! A famous person to come and bless the place with their presence, listen to my woeful tale, and leave a tip for fifty-thousand dollars.

I sigh audibly. No one remotely popular ever comes to Bristlemouth Bay.

"Maybe I could help," Greg offers.

"You're not supposed to talk." I've been painfully aware of him, sitting next to me, his thigh pressed against mine. They say you never get over your first love. Sounds true enough. A snapshot of our first time together before it went south suddenly appears, and my heart aches fresh.

He ignores my reminder. "Remember when we met and you were wondering if you should go off-island and have your hair dyed? You wanted to try turquoise, but your mom said you were too young and it would be bad for business. And I said—"

"—Just tell me every angle of the story, and see what you come up with," I finish for him.

It helped a lot, having an ear, as I worked the problem out aloud. Greg didn't offer advice or push an opinion. He just let me hash out a pros and cons list. Before long, I figured out my thoughts on the matter.

I never did get my hair dyed, but I'm not sure if it was because my mother would have made my life a living hell the way she does with my minor acts of rebellion or because Greg liked the natural sun-bleached color so much. He would let the strands fall through his fingers as we sat by the fires on the beach and "get lost in its shine"—his words.

What do I have to lose by sharing my turmoil with Greg? He already took every shred of dignity away from me by dumping me soon after giving him my "most precious gift"—my mother's words.

I tell him everything, right down to how often I've spoken to a pair of urns and how, at times, believed my grandparents responded. When he asks why I'm dating an "old man," I explain the bizarre hold Steve has on my parents, knowing they won't turn away a stranger in need and how he uses it to his full advantage.

Finally, we discuss tonight.

"I'm so grateful you and Brandon were close by. Never would I have suspected Steve would have tried something like that. He mostly ignores me when he comes over, just sucks up to my parents." I snort. "Come to think of it, now that I know the whole story, I bet he comes to lord the loan over them.

"God! What a putz! I wish the crowd had thrown *him* over the wall."

The conductor announces our stop, and we gather our things before disembarking.

I take Greg by the arm outside on the platform, stopping him momentarily to let the other passengers pass by.

"Thank you for helping me and for being so unlike the

Steve's of the world. I wouldn't have made it home without you."

"We're not there yet." He twines his fingers with mine as we head over to Greg's ride—Jack's new truck. I'd recognize it anywhere. Being a true islander, I notice the particulars about the other residents' lives.

Greg holds the passenger door open for me before rounding the massive machine and jumping in. He strokes my ego when he leans slightly in, saying, "I think you're brave for facing the restaurant situation head-on."

"But you agree that harassing the citizens of Bristlemouth might be a waste of time?"

As always, he lets me own the solution, the tilt of his head noncommittal.

"Mmm! That new car smell!" I let him off the hook when I notice.

Greg turns on the air conditioner, which intensifies the delicious odor.

We both breathe deeply, trying to inhale enough to save for later.

He keeps the truck in park and angles himself toward me. "Lia, I should have done this sooner. I should have been a man, knocked on your door, and just said it. I'm sorry. I know I made you doubt yourself when I broke up with you."

I let him talk. After waiting four years for this apology, I'm going to enjoy it and end the day on a positive note.

"I kinda lost it when I found out who my dad was—nothing was the same. I took it out on everyone: you, my mom." He shakes his head. "It felt like everyone and everything was a lie. I couldn't hack it."

His dark look thrills me the way it used to.

"I enjoyed our night together more than anything I've ever done before or since," he concludes.

I snort, as is my way. It's a character flaw I've had difficulty controlling at times.

"Yeah. Yeah. You're a guy. Of course it's your favorite."

He pauses, collecting his thoughts. "No, Lia. That night was the greatest of my life because it was with *you.*"

The regret in his expression is naked and honest; I fight tears from forming. I'm not sure what I'm supposed to say, but I'm not going to tell him how deeply he hurt me. How I haven't had a serious boyfriend since. Or that I haven't—

Suffice to say I'm not telling him anything about me regarding that one memorable night. Still, I appreciate the apology and that sentiment I do share.

"Thanks, Greg. It means a lot to hear you apologize." I place my hand over his and lean over to kiss his cheek.

He catches me by surprise when my lips land on his.

Pushing back slightly, I ask, "Did you learn that move from Steve?"

Good-naturedly, he laughs. "I deserve that."

But his mouth feels so good, nothing at all like Steve's fish-face pucker, and I want more. I want him as I always have. Better than just smelling him, I taste him: minty, manly, and all Greg.

Our kiss deepens as my hands splay across his chest and his fingers wind through my hair. Knowing a relationship isn't an option—Greg has already proven himself a fly-by kind of guy, and my life is in too great a state of flux—I enjoy this moment for what it is and continue to reminisce with my hands and my mouth all we have and shared.

We reach a stage where it's either stop or take your clothes off, and I choose to end it without being caught this time. With a few closing pecks, I push back onto my seat and ask, "Ready to go home, Greg?"

It's obvious he'd rather say "no," but as a gentleman,

instead, he nods, repositions himself in his seat, and puts the truck in drive. "Yep, pretty sure Jack would kill me if I got his truck seats sticky."

What else could I do but laugh? And all the way home, our hands found reason to connect—like magnets destined for one another.

5

LIA

Think. Think. Think. My teeth dig deep into the pencil held between my index finger and thumb as I consider the next logical step, leaning back in the office chair. I won't have my father accusing me of thinking like a "girl" or my mother admonishing, "You wear your heart on your sleeve!"

Why can't adults remember when they were young and everything felt overwhelming and out of reach?

So I don't lose a tooth in the graphite, I remove the writing tool from my mouth and swing it up and down between my index and middle finger, tapping a rhythm on the paper-strewn desk. I've been working on the loan problem for hours now with nothing to show but a clear cast of my denti-tion, useful only for a forensics investigation.

After talking to Greg after the baseball game fiasco, I decided a pity party wouldn't get me anywhere. He has this way of helping me focus on the fundamentals so I don't get lost in fantasy. "It's all in the consistent micro-steps. No leaping allowed!"

He smelled the way I remembered. When he pulled his

little maneuver, landing a kiss, my appetite revved up, insatiable.

I haven't dated much since he left, but it's not like I've stayed home, either. But no matter how wide a net you cast in this tiny hamlet, you pull in the same characters. Some men are looking for one thing. Others treat you as if women's liberation permitted them to slam doors in your face should you dare to go out looking less than runway ready. And don't get me started on the pictures they send. *Put it away, boys. No one wants to see that!*

So many dates made me pay for dinner or split the bill under the guise of equality. No, it's cheap, and you're a cheapskate.

Greg's different. As young as we were, and still are, he acts like a man—a real one. The kind who doesn't just get the door; he shows up at your door and escorts you back safely at the end of the night. He picks up the tab unless you scheme days in advance to curtail the waitress and grab the check. Though it's never been necessary, I have no doubt he'd be willing to remove his coat and drape it over a puddle if need be.

After explaining this to my friend Tanya, she said, "That's nice, but don't you like a little edge? You know, the bad boy who seems unattainable." Her eyes glittered bright, and I knew she was thinking about Devon, the new bartender. He's handsome and moody and hardly says a word, but he rides a motorcycle and hooks up with lonely women who roam into the bar on Saturday nights.

"You mean an asshole?"

She blushed and admitted, "Kinda."

I shook my head and allowed her opinion. That's what friends do when there's no changing them.

Plus, she doesn't know Greg does have an edge, an

energy he contains and controls because he's the real deal. Knowing Tanya would never understand or appreciate what I meant, I had let the topic lie. Besides, I didn't want her to decide to investigate. He might not be mine, but I certainly wasn't going to hand him over to her, or anyone else for that matter.

Right now, I force myself from daydreaming about cuddling up close on the train or kissing him in the truck. Mmm, it's tough, but I return to the task at hand and pull out the only tool left in my arsenal: my journal.

Swinging my legs off the desk, I sit upright in the chair and pull the history of my life out of my bag and allow it to open to whichever page it lands.

Since I began waiting tables at ten years old, I've been using it as a diary of sorts. Inside are all the stories and photos my parents and the others from the restaurant and community and guests have shared, reminders of memories I cherish.

One of the best parts of restaurant work in a touristy area is meeting people who visit from all over the world. On top of endless guests from all fifty states, Canada, and Mexico, I have names and information about visitors from England, Africa, Japan, Australia, and many places in between.

What fascinates me about distant, exotic places isn't monuments or history or anything significant like that, but how the world appears outside their windows. The first thing they see in the morning and the last the view at night. Do they have a garden teaming with vegetables and perennials, a yard with green rolling hills, or a mountain in the distance?

People tend to be so happy on vacation, and they love to share their stories. Many guests have stayed in touch through texts and email, and some send pictures, helping me visualize what life in their corner of the world is like.

Second to running the business, the only thing that would have come close as a profession is being a traveling journalist, a photojournalist in particular. It's a shame that would entail college, and we're broke.

Turning page after page, many with photographs taped alongside my notes, the walk down memory lane has me smiling.

Karoline visited from Norway, and she gave me my first tube of lipgloss on my eleventh birthday. Bubblegum flavored, I kept the container well after it was empty to pull off the cap and let the scent take me back. She was tall, blond, and striking in that Norse way. The picture she shared was the Northern Lights as seen from her bedroom window.

Sakura was my age and lived with her parents in Japan, her father a much sought-after shrine craftsman. Bubbly and carefree, we spent a day together at the beach. As much of a tomboy as me, we filled our time mucking for clams, chasing Fidler crabs back into the water, and bodysurfing in the waves. After returning home, she sent me a brass Rin Gong, a Japanese singing bowl. It sits on a red and yellow silk cushion displayed on the shelves behind the desk where I sit.

I swivel my chair and hit the edge with the striker, the sound fills the space, inviting relaxation and reflection.

Next is Noa, who lived in Maui. A surfer to the bone, he was my first real crush. Tall and tanned to a rich ebony color, he always made time to greet me when he came to the restaurant to pick up take out with his petite and stunning wife, Iolani. She was so small in stature I convinced my twelve-year-old self she was his daughter and not his wife. Forget that she was six months pregnant, and the photo he shared was of her sonogram!

These memories bring me back to a yesterday a dozen years in the making.

I'm considering texting and emailing those who could help. One of my past buddies might know someone famous or may have become famous, or maybe they won the lottery and have gobs of money to spare. I haven't fully decided because it feels presumptuous and rude. Haven't they shared enough by sending their stories and pictures? Still, the answer's always no if you don't ask.

It's a lot to think about. I need a break. I've spent the last week living in the office, sleeping on the couch, and taking my meals at the desk. My back hurts from sitting too long, and my belly calls out for more food.

I rise and stretch, blurry from low blood sugar and lack of sleep, and allow thoughts of Greg to sustain me as I head to the kitchen to rustle up something to eat.

I say his name out loud, my fantasy powerful, when his apparition holds the wrong side of the kitchen doors. Even for a phantom, he's lucky. Nothing pisses off waitstaff more than someone who doesn't stick to the right side when entering and exiting a busy kitchen. We've all been burned, and it leaves scars.

Unwilling to let a pleasant dream pass by, I walk up, bold as I wish because it's my hallucination, and kiss his sexy mouth, full and deep.

I'm pleasantly shocked when the real Greg deepens the kiss, pulling me hard against his worn T-shirt.

Greg

Her gray pallor makes it look like Lia has been indoors for the better part of the summer and not simply avoiding the places I've been frequenting.

Since the night at Fenway, I've changed tactics. Instead of making sure the coast is clear, I look for excuses to see her. It turns out I have more luck when I try to avoid her and less when I actively seek. The bonfire and carnival nights were boring without her, and I gave up going after a couple of times.

She walks as if in a trance toward the kitchen. The same place I just left a stack of pastry boxes.

So engrossed, Lia bumps into me when I pull the kitchen door open, and she kisses me. What else could I do but kiss her back?

"Greg!" She jerks in surprise as she causes the same reaction in me when she plants a kiss on my lips.

I don't hold back. I pull her so close she rises on tiptoes, taking all she has to offer in a public venue before releasing her feet steady back on the floor.

What I wouldn't give to have my own place to suggest we head over to. Indeed, neither the couch where I'm crashing at Jack and my mom's or the well-equipped break room at the lab seem viable options.

"Lia. I'm glad I ran into you."

"Oh, yeah?" Her skin flushes a healthier shade and she glows.

"Clara sent me with your first delivery, and every other day until further notice she claims. I just left them on the prep table."

Her eyes round as she swallows hard. "Okay. Thanks."

"I'll grab the rest from the car. Clara lent me hers for the errand with the bonus that I could hang onto it for the rest of the day. It's good to have generous relatives close by to barter a loaner."

Getting no response, I shrug and head back out to the car. When I return with the six pies—two apple, two cherry, and two Boston cream—Lia is leaning on the opposite counter finishing a cream-filled chocolate cupcake with ganache frosting. If it weren't for the missing piping of white squiggles, Aunt Clara might have to answer to the Hostess company.

Wishing to go back to where we bumped into each other, I snag a carrot cake cupcake with cream cheese frosting and join Lia against the counter. "So, how about that greeting?"

She mumbles behind her dessert.

"What was that?"

"I was hungry for—" she pauses and walks over to the refrigerator to fill two glasses with milk. She hands one to me on her return and finishes the dodge. "Chocolate. I was craving it."

"I've never made out with a dessert, so I really can't speak to the desire. Is it everything you wanted?"

Casually, she grabs another cupcake and begins eating it from the top without removing the paper. "Mostly. Until I want another." After another massive bite, she swallows says, "And another."

Brandon picks the worst and best moment to show up for his shift, breaking the flirtatious atmosphere. The worst because I hoped to flirt her right back up against me, and the best as I had no volley left to send.

The flirtation gene must share the science geek chromosome because as straightforward as studying is for me, so is the difficulty of creating fun comebacks.

"Hey, guys," Brandon greets us casually, walking between us to grab a cupcake. "Mmm! Clara's?"

"Yup," I tell him, pushing away from the counter. "I better get going. Jack needs me to gather cheek swabs at the library on my way back to the lab. The genealogy group meets today, and they're hoping to find something distinctive to brag about."

Brandon looks first at Lia's face, then mine, picking up too late that he walked in on something.

"You've got frosting on your chin," he tells Lia.

A tiny chocolate dot is the only blemish on her pretty face.

"And you, my friend, have it up your nose." He pulls his ball cap on backward and ties his apron before pulling down pots and pans from the hooks above the stove.

Horrified, I check and find a gob of the stuff inside the left nostril. With Lia standing to my right, she wouldn't have seen it if he hadn't pointed it out, and in one split second, I've gone from being the cool guy with the right things to say, who brings the chocolate when only chocolate will do, to remaining the idiot who was fool enough to let her go.

My plan to get the girl back lies in shambles as she heads back to the office, and I drive to the library to play with other people's spit—and not anyone's I care to.

6

GREG

R.E.M. plays on the radio, cranked high, helping us stay awake.

Seven hours of running D.N.A test after D.N.A test leaves the eyes dry and the lines on the test strip blurry. Everyone starts looking like they're related, which technically is true, only not in a relative way. (It's a geneticist joke; relative having multiple meanings.) Once you hit six or so generations, it no longer matters.

With only one hour left in the workday, Jack focuses on the computer side while I finish running the rest of the labs. Ryder rests fitfully. The tide in his dream must be high and full of waves.

Jack turns down the music. "Hey, did I ever tell you I met Gino Lawson? Ran his strip a few years ago before he hit it big."

"Who?" I ask, not recognizing the name.

"Gino Lawson," he utters slowly. "The star of *Moonlight Melody*."

I shake my head, still at a loss.

"The nighttime soap opera where all the characters live on

the moon. President Poseidon, played by Gino, was a ballroom dancer when he lived on earth. They fight the evils of space and time. Mainly, it's a bunch of beautiful people who claim to have found the fountain of youth."

Playing along, I ask, "Which is?"

"Near as I can tell, sex. And dancing the salsa, samba, or swing every chance they get."

He's serious.

"This isn't a joke? You watch this show?"

"Me?" he points at his chest with a pen shaped like a hypodermic needle. "No. But your Uncle Gabe and Alicia love it. They say it's the B-list show to end all B-list shows—a so bad its funny sort of thing.

"I was thinking about Lia's problem. What if I could get Gino to visit The Clam Digger? He's quite popular with women over childbearing age."

"So your fan base?"

"Pretty much," he accedes. "You want me to text him? Ask if he's got some free time?"

"I don't know, Jack. He sounds lame." I shake my head at the lunacy, knowing I have to watch the show now. "I think Lia was hoping for Brad Pitt or Bradley Cooper in a pinch, not a dancing lunar leader."

Jack walks up beside me and hands me my phone. "Call her. She can decide."

I roll my eyes and take the phone. She's going to think I'm more of a clod than before, but I'm glad to have a reason to talk to her.

Our interactions this summer have been few but filled with fiery little surprises. Sweet and reserved is how I would describe the Lia I dated four years ago. Her newly adopted forward approach and confident air are doubly enticing. Still, as alluring as being her secret make-out buddy is, I'm looking for more. Maybe there's still a chance for us. Not forever; we're only twenty-two, but…

It's sad how Gino Lawson is the only idea I've come up with in a month to really grab her attention. Technically the plan belongs to Jack, but she hasn't been around at any of her regular spots. Lia used to hit up every celebration, like fireworks on July fourth and Friday night concerts at Flora's Field, but working on saving the business has her locked inside the office 24/7.

She answers on the third ring. "Hi, Greg."

"Hi, um, Lia." Sudden congestion in my throat has my voice sounding thready and high. Clearing it, I continue, "I hope you don't mind. I shared a bit of your story with Jack. He has this weird idea that if he could get this guy, Gino Lawson, to come to Bristlemouth, you might raise some money that way."

A heavy pause follows my suggestion. *I knew it!* Gino Lawson is a nobody.

I'm about to apologize and hang up when she shrieks at the end of the line.

"Are you kidding me? *The* Gino Lawson? President Poseidon, the Passion of the Penumbra?"

The sound of the show somehow just got worse. "You know about him?" *The Passion of the Penumbra?* Who the hell writes this crap, and why is everyone watching it?

"Yes!" She's as excited as I've ever heard her. "Brandon, Melissa, and Tanya come over every Thursday nigh, so we can watch it together. We turned it into a drinking game. Every time someone turns their head, shooting their gaze dramatically to the side of the room or out a window, you have to take a drink. Whenever a character forces a kiss that melts into a make-out session—and they all do—you drink twice. If a chest, male or female heaves, and you don't yell,

'Heaving bosom!', you have to finish whatever's left in your glass. And whenever Poseidon initiates an impromptu dance party, you have to shotgun a can of beer.

"Some weeks we get so drunk, they have to call a cab or walk home, but usually they just end up staying over so we can laugh the rest of the night, reliving the horrid acting and sappy lines."

What a relief! I was afraid for a second she might actually like the show.

"So, I take it your answer is yes."

"A thousand yes's!" She sounds like a preteen at a One Direction concert. "Will Jack text him now? Like, right this second?"

She's so loud, Jack's fingers already fly over his phone's keyboard.

"Done!" he proclaims. "Now we wait."

"Tell him there isn't much time, Greg. If he says yes, I'll need to take out an ad in the local papers and talk to the news and radio stations. This is so exciting," she squeals, then her voice goes soft. "Do you think I could meet him beforehand? For a private dance lesson?

"Oh my God! I have to call my Thursday crew! They'll want to be a part of this, I'm sure.

"Greg, you are the best. I'm so happy. Please let me know the second you hear back. I gotta fly and call those guys or I'll bust. I'm blowing you two kisses over the phone. Share one of those with Jack." And with that, she's gone.

"So, not so out of touch for an old guy, am I?"

"No, Jack, you're mad modern," I respond in a distracted fashion.

He gloats and asks me to turn up the radio volume to hear the weather report.

Why didn't Lia invite me to a show night? It seems the

least she could do after how happy she was to hear the news. Maybe she's waiting to ask once Lawson agrees. Or maybe our interludes meant nothing to her and she's moved on from the more innocent time.

I'm more confused than before I made the call about convincing Lia we're a good idea. She's busy, and I'll be leaving soon for school, so realistically I should probably let go of the hope. I just don't want to.

Lia

He said yes! I sing it in my head every moment I'm awake. *Gino Lawson said yes! Gino Lawson said yes!*

And life hasn't been the same since. It's like *I'm* the television star. When I greet people at the hostess station or take orders at tables, they keep asking, "So, when is Gino coming? Have you spoken to him yet? What's he like? I hear he's approachable."

The answer is the same. "August twentieth. Yes, we spoke for ten minutes. He's incredible! Funny, fascinating, and wicked down to earth!"

Nothing exciting ever happens in Bristlemouth Bay—until now. And we are going to soak up every minute we can, starting tonight. The festivities will kick off at six o'clock with my parents hosting a clambake and *Moonlight Melody* showing. On a continuous loop, the show will play all three seasons.

Dad even made up a specialty drink (one-part black vodka, two parts Kahlúa, watered down with club soda, and decorated with a gray-colored rock candy swizzle stick) at fifteen bucks a glass.

To access the bar and its libations, you must partake in the silly *Moonlight Melody* game we play. Brandon, Tanya, and Melissa are going to hand out instructions at the door, and a fleet of taxis will idle in the parking lot to drive people home when they head out.

❧

The entire town, it seems, came, and all night the space has been stuffed to the gills with everyone dancing, singing, and mimicking iconic moments of the show as it plays on the widescreen TV over the bar.

After tonight, I'll be known forever as the person who made all this happen, but more importantly, The Clam Digger will be mine!

In addition to bankrolling the wild party, Gino promised to eat every meal in the restaurant during his two-day stay, *and* he's going to teach a dance class right inside the banquet room. I'm going to be his partner! Life does not get better than this.

Tickets for the upcoming dance sold out faster than those for tonight's bash. Every available seat is reserved morning, noon, and night, and even though it's a few days until he arrives, the restaurant has been busting at the seams with patrons for the past two weeks. We're turning the highest profits in the restaurant's history before Gino even gets on a plane.

That, my friends, is true star power!

Too quickly, it's that time in a party where people get sloppy. As I cinch my apron tighter to my hips, Pete Granger, the town treasurer, swivels on his barstool and spills his drink down the front of me.

Slurring, he apologizes while trying to clean me up with his bare hand—up and down my soaking wet chest.

Up goes my trusty food tray, and the friendly guy with the big drinking problem pets the flat surface, still trying to clean up. If it was anyone else, I'd hit them over the head with the tray, but Pete is always polite and never says an unkind word about anyone when he's sober. He's just lost in his disease.

"I'm sorry, Lia. It's time for me to go." His breath is wet in my ear as I catch him when he stumbles after taking his first step.

"It's okay, Pete. We'll get you home." I wave down Brandon as he exits the kitchen. The lights go dark behind him as the door swings closed.

Seeing my struggle, he hurries over to take Pete's weight off my shoulder.

"Thanks, Brandon."

Pete almost slips away, but Brandon catches him at the last minute and tosses Pete's arm across his shoulders.

"No problem. Can you make sure I locked the back door while I help Pete into a cab?"

"If you check on Carole next."

Brandon looks at the farthest barstool, knowing she'd be in "her" spot. Pete's third wife, Carole, sits slumped over the bar, her long, gray, frizzy hair floating in the remnants of her whisky sour.

"Yup. I'll circle the room after I get them both situated and put anyone else who's had too much into a cab." And with that, the two men stumble toward the front door in the age-old shuffle of strong sober guy helping weak drunk guy get home safely.

Walking to the kitchen, I remove my soiled apron and find my wet blouse clings suggestively to my bra, showing the world I picked a lacy, pale pink number tonight. I shrug.

Everyone is drunk and disoriented. I'll grab a new apron and no one will be any the wiser.

Without the overheads, the lighting is dim, cast from a small globe over the sink. The sound from the TV cuts out as the door swings closed, and I hear my dad announce the bar officially closed. "Party's over, folks. Thanks for coming."

I know that he and my mom will stand by the doors to ensure no one gets past Brandon's keen eye and accidentally tries to drive home drunk. Then they'll head up to bed, leaving the rest of the cleanup to me and the remaining staff.

The refrigerator motor kicks on as I pass it to the back door. I jump, startled, which makes me laugh because it's a sound I've heard a thousand times before.

"Get a grip, Lia. You've gone Mooney," I joke out loud to soothe myself. Too many episodes of *Moonlight Melody* have me thinking of drama and intrigue.

I twist the metal doorknob in my hand and find it and the deadbolt above are already locked. Of course it is. Brandon takes better care of the kitchen than I do of my bedroom. He tells all the sous chefs, "A clean kitchen is the only kitchen I'll tolerate."

Before I can turn to grab a fresh apron off the hook to help Devon prep the bar for tomorrow, a large hand covers my mouth, and another clutches at my belly, pulling me close.

"Just let me touch you. No one has to know."

7

GREG

Finally, I'm invited to a *Moonlight Melody* night, and I show up with zinnias for Lia and two bottles of wine for the group, only to discover the whole town at The Clam Digger having a blast.

My hope was to take Brandon aside while we watched the show in Lia's tiny apartment over the restaurant, encourage him to leave with Tanya and Melissa, and have Lia to myself. If I stick to that strategy, Brandon will have to find a way to lure two hundred people away without Lia suspecting anything.

So it's back to the drawing board. I'll walk on the beach, wait for the crowd to disperse, and sneak in the back door. Using the element of surprise, I'll catch Lia off guard and tell her exactly how I feel. How I've missed her. How thinking of her fills my every waking moment. How desperate I am to touch her, hold her, and love her again.

But everything I come up with sounds stupid.

After cracking open a bottle of red and taking a hearty slug, I sit still on a flat rock and watch the slack tide. A few minutes pass, and things begin to stir as crabs exit their burrows to feed. The full moon casts shadows off their sideways, stiff-legged ballet; the show helps me relax.

Words still escape me, but actions speak louder than words as the adage goes, and those ideas flood in. It takes a while, but soon I have a plan to sweep her off her feet.

In the distance, revelers exit the restaurant and cars, mostly taxis, drive out of the parking lot. It's time for action, and I jog to the rear entrance and slip inside the backdoor.

Someone's coming! My attempt at hiding behind a bunch of aprons fails when I bang my head against the pegs from which they hang. Spying a narrow door three feet away, I lunge and pull it open, closing it tight behind me simultaneous to Lia, saying, "Get a grip, Lia. You've gone Mooney."

I roll my eyes at the catchphrase and then remember why I'm here. Taking a deep breath, I prepare to grab the girl and lay one on her. Would she prefer to be held by the shoulders or from the hip area?

I think back and recall the kiss at the kitchen door. Besides my mouth, my body wasn't touching her at all. Then again, when she kissed me after the game, our hands were moving so fast I hardly remember which body part I *didn't* touch.

No. I need to touch her. My hands, her shoulders, our lips. I'll roam from there.

Jiggling the knob, I discover it's stuck. She'll be gone in a second, and I'll be sleeping in a stockroom all night.

Lia checks the lock on the back door, and I question whether it will look unmanly to knock and ask for help when another voice speaks.

❧

Lia

Forget the disturbing voice, the taut, round beer gut pressing firmly against my back, and the smell of his fetid breath; it's the clamminess of Steve's hands that give him away. A cold slimy sensation smears across my cheek as I struggle out of his grip.

I wipe my face vigorously to get the creep off my skin and spit into a nearby slop sink. "Yuck! Don't you ever touch me!"

Ignoring my command, Steve pushes me against the wall. "I just want to give—" The sentence cuts off with a wild shriek as my knee strikes him hard as a hammer blow between his legs. Coughing, he lands on his knees before falling sideways on the floor, curled in a fetal position.

"I warned you." I stand over him and release my frustration. "You don't listen! No one likes you. No one wants you around. And I'm keeping the restaurant if it's the last thing I do! Got it?"

Weakly, he holds up an antique ring with a small ruby in the center and chokes out, "Marry me."

"What?" I'd be less freaked out if he were brandishing a gun.

"Then we both win." He belly crawls toward me, still clutching his wounded member.

Grabbing a nearby broom, I swat him over the back with it and yell, "You're a psycho. Get out."

"No," he says, stumbling to his feet.

Surprising us both, the alcohol pantry door slams open behind him, and Greg shoots out, almost hitting the opposite wall in his haste to rescue me.

Steve asks no questions, just bolts for the door. He fumbles with the locks, keening like a wild animal pursued by a predator, and storms out into the rear parking lot.

I reach past Greg and lock the door behind him. Leaning

against it, I catch my breath before asking Greg, "And what the hell are you doing here?"

He hides his groin area behind a bottle of wine. "I came to see you and got accidentally locked inside. When I saw you through the slats in the door, I didn't know what to make of it at first. It seemed maybe you two were a "thing," but then you kicked him." Greg's grimace mirrors the one Steve wore. "You've got a helluva hip flexor there."

I roll my eyes and walk toward him. Men! Such a weak spot.

Greg picks a bouquet of flowers off the floor and thrusts them my way, still nervous about my approach.

I take the colorful bunch, toss them on the stainless steel prep table, and grab the wine bottle instead. "Screw top?"

"I've never bought wine before."

"Gets the job done."

Staring Greg in the eye, I unscrew the cap and swill. The taste of Steve lingers, and I consume more. Eventually, my head swims from the alcohol shunting through my liver, and I feel less eww.

The fast pace of my drinking leaves me breathless, and I watch as Greg's eyes lose their battle with respect and dart down to my wet blouse. How is it one man's gaze can repulse and another ignite?

Softly, Greg notes, "Heaving bosom."

Game rules stipulate I must drink, and I do. Then I toss the empty bottle into the trash and lunge at Greg. My hands twine in his thick, dark hair. My lips latch onto his as my legs wrap around his waist.

Young, fit, and powerful, he catches my weight without missing a beat.

My thighs cling tight, allowing him to touch me wherever he wishes, the same way I explore his body. His face nuzzles between my breasts, and the top two buttons of my shirt pop open, encouraging.

I pull at the bottom of his shirt and touch the fiery skin of his abdomen. Muscle by muscle, I march my fingertips up his torso until I pull the shirt off entirely.

He pushes the flowers off the tabletop and replaces them with my bum. Instantly, he removes my blouse, and his tongue darts beneath the cup of my bra to tease my nipple into growing harder than it was. Skillfully, he releases the clasp in the back, removing the bit of fabric along with the rest of our reserve.

He cups both breasts in his warm, dry hands, reverently. "You're so beautiful, Lia. I wish—"

I shut him up with a kiss. He's going to bring up the night of our first time, and I don't want the visual. "Please, Greg," I beg. "Just this. Just now."

Sitting on the razor's edge of the table, it's easy to hook my foot around his hips and pull him closer. The action breaks his thoughts, and he crushes his groin against mine, moaning in ecstasy, "Oh God, Lia."

"I want you, Greg."

Tugging at his pants, he helps me assist their fall to the floor.

"Everyone's gone home," I continue to assure him.

No need to take my bottoms off; I wore a skirt to work. Smooth and steady, his palms side the length of my legs until his index fingers hook around the strings of my bikini, and with one quick tug, they disappear.

"No one is going to interrupt us."

We're as close as two humans can be, nothing separating our joining except the overhead light that just flickered on. The buzz from the fluorescents heating up matches the hornet's nest in my brain.

Not again!

Brandon doesn't see us at first, with the high ledge of the prep table hiding us until he rounds the corner. There, he can see everything.

Greg thinks fast and pulls me closer, so even if Brandon looked, all he would see is the side of my nude torso and thigh and Greg's muscly arms wrapping around them.

But Brandon isn't like that. He's polite, kind, and a true friend. After a "Whoa!" and a "Shit!" from him as he covers his eyes with his hands, the three of us crack up laughing.

"Sorry, you two. I forgot my apartment keys. Moved into the new place, and now with the," he mumbles something incoherent and finishes with, "Well, whatever." Brandon sneaks past us with his back turned, grabs the keys from the windowsill, and bids us adieu.

Greg still holds me close, but the mood has definitely broken. Though it's a relief to be caught by a friend this time, somehow, it extinguishes the passion just the same.

We kiss slow and tender and sweet before Greg gathers our clothes and divvies them between us.

"Were you afraid Brandon might look?" Greg asks as he steps into his pants and shoves his feet inside his sneakers.

"No. And I wouldn't care if he did."

Greg stops dressing and looks out at me through the neck of his shirt, stuck halfway down his head.

"What? Why not?"

"Because he's gay."

He yanks his shirt fully on and cocks his head to the side. "He's what?"

"Gay."

"Gay? What?" Surprise has Greg incapable of comprehending the obvious fact about our friend. "How so?"

"By being gay, I mean that he likes men, Greg. Take you, for instance."

He points to his chest, mouth agape. "I'm not gay."

I smile and help him straighten his rumpled outfit. "No. You definitely like women. But why do you think Brandon invited you to that bonfire your first summer? Non-residents are never invited. We told you that."

"I helped him with his bike."

"He was hoping you were gay."

"Really?"

"Sure. You're gorgeous, trim, fastidious, and tremendously polite."

"That makes you gay?" he teases.

"No!" I smack his arm. "He realized his mistake right after you went, as he puts it, 'All goofy' on me."

"So that was supposed to be a date?"

"Yup. You broke his heart, but he fell in love with you anyway. The same way I—" I busy myself with the last buttons on my blouse, disbelieving what I was about to say. "Love chocolate." I cover my tracks like a pro. "Come on. I'll walk you out."

"Only to the door. Then lock it behind me quick as you can. That Steve guy is unpredictable."

I lift my knee between Greg's legs to pantomime what I'm capable of. Instead of causing agony, I make him groan.

"I've got skills I don't mind sharing," I whisper in his ear.

A pleasant thrill runs through us both as we exchange a final kiss goodnight.

"Until next time?" Greg asks.

"Sure," I agree with my fingers crossed behind my back that the next time is before he leaves for school. Then I lock the door behind him.

8

LIA

Not even the threatening clouds hanging heavy in the sky can make me gloomy today.

I thought I had it all with everything working toward saving the restaurant and hosting the island's first celebrity, but last night Greg reminded me what I was lacking all along; the zing and yowza a new relationship brings.

What was I hiding from all these past summers? Greg ticks off all my boxes, and I've behaved like a child. I should have gone right up to him and said—

What could I have said? I shrug and figure anything would have been better than nothing.

The dining room darkens without warning. Outside, the clouds thicken and roll, billowing toward earth like waves of molten lava instead of floating away to another land, making rain a guarantee.

Getting my head out of the clouds, I grab a pitcher of water and greet the guests at table six before filling their glasses. It reminds me of the flowers I rescued from the floor after Greg left last night. The deep crimson, hot pink, and crisp white zinnias now sit on my bedside table in a vase. I fell asleep and woke to their beauty, a visual reminder of Greg's touch and tender approach.

"That should about do it, dear."

Distracted with thoughts of him pressed against me, I barely hear Reverend Carmichael whose glass I'm filling.

"What can I get you?" I ask, my thoughts still on Greg and his strong arms, holding my weight as he transferred me to the prep table like two Hollywood stars nailing the most incredible love scene of all time.

"Yipe!" Belinda yells and stands to let the water sluice off her lap.

"Oh, shit! I mean shoot, Reverend." I grab a stack of napkins from another table and, along with the two women she's having lunch with, help her clean up.

My eyes grow wide, and I clench my jaw as I bravely face the holy woman. "Sorry, I swore."

"I've said worse. Jesus forgives our human frailties." She sits back down and spreads a clean napkin over her lap before placing her order for clam strips and onion rings.

Her friends make my life easy and order the same.

Belinda pats my hand gently. "We all have our heads in the clouds today."

The reverend couldn't be sweeter, but I always feel sinful and hedonistic for being a practicing nothing. My parents never went to church, and most of what I know about Jesus comes from the show *South Park*. Jesus might forgive a swear or two, but will he be okay with me shaking Belinda and the other churchgoers down for donations? I remember the phone conversation and recall that Belinda offered to pass around the collection plate.

Relieved, I wipe my brow with the soiled stack of napkins, sure I won't be struck down if the storm brewing outside contains lightning.

I tell the ladies, "It's on the house," and hurry off to submit the order.

I overhear Mary talking to a few regulars about the weather on my way past the bar. I'll never understand the fascination. You wanna know what it's doing outside? Look outside. Go outside. Simple. Except what I overheard sounded complex.

"What did you just say, Mary?"

"The town council is weighing the pros and cons about evacuating."

"Evacuating what?"

"Us," she says, spreading her arms to include everyone in the room. "The island. Don't you listen to the weather?"

"No."

Ralph, who has been the island mailman since the town was incorporated (not factual, but he received an award for being Bristlemouth's oldest resident two years ago when he turned 100), pats my hand, "You're too young to focus on boring stuff. When's President What's-His-Name arriving?"

I open my mouth to answer questions about my favorite topic when Mary cuts me off. "Your parents are already packing."

"For what?"

"They aren't waiting for the evacuation order. After the last report, your mom said, 'Enough's enough with this shit! Sam, I'm going to Florida for good this time. You coming?' I'm assuming it was a yes because he followed her after putting up that flyer." She points to the front window.

Reading the words written in black magic marker backward, it says, "Closed until further notice."

What?

"The hurricane they thought was heading out to sea might take a sharp left turn over Bristlemouth Bay instead. It may be a Category 4 or 5 by the time it hits the shore. Once it hits the Worcester Hills, it'll slow to a 1 or 2."

"Good for them," says Minnie, the last pastor's widow. She's a bit senile, but with her devoted daughter Gertie forever by her side, she does well enough.

Gertie pats Minnie's arm and tries to get her to finish her meal.

"We're screwed!" calls out Jim, the town curmudgeon. He says that about everything from mosquitoes to the tourists that keep businesses in Bristlemouth open.

"You better go talk to him. Sam said the flight leaves Logan in three hours."

I untie my apron and run upstairs, discovering it's all true. My parents frantically pack as my mother calls out orders. "Don't forget the umbrella! No, not that one, the one that looks like a Monet. I'll grab the hairdryer."

"Mom? Dad?"

Dad stops to explain while my mom runs into the adjoining bathroom to fill up her carry-on with toiletries.

"I was just about to come find you. Pack up. We're leaving in thirty minutes."

"I can't leave. Gino Lawson arrives in two days, remember?"

Mom strides back into the room. "Oh, honey. That was nothing but a pipe dream. Even if he came, do you honestly think he would have brought in enough money to save the place?"

Her words slap me in the face. I gave up hoping for a nurturing mother long ago, but to tell me no one believed I could do this is decidedly harsh.

I defend my case. "Well, no, but a lot. And when you add it to what I've already accrued—"

She's not listening, but I'd hoped to talk to the lawyers

about how quickly I raised ten thousand dollars to see if we could renegotiate. Also, I planned to hit it off so well with Gino he'd come back for a Christmas encore.

"I'm proud of myself, Mom." I swipe at tears with my wrist, embarrassed she can cut me with a simple phrase.

"You did great, honey," she rubs my arm on the way out of the bedroom door, my father pulling multiple suitcases down the hall behind her. I hustle to keep up. "You can take those skills anywhere, and right now, you're taking them to Florida." She rounds the corner and bounds down the stairs to exit the rear of the restaurant to the employee parking lot and dumpster area.

I hope this doesn't turn into a hair-dye moment, us on different sides, both willing to fight. I'm not giving in this time.

"No, Mom. I'm staying. I'm seeing this to the bitter end, no matter what the result."

She surprises me, beams her brightest smile, her eyes misting up. "Sam, did we raise a brave and independent girl or what?"

Hm. No argument? I pick up on her desire to wrap this up when she rolls her hand in the universal sign of "let's go" at my father.

"What's your hurry?" I ask, my feelings hurting a touch that they'd prefer to be dry than by my side when I'm victorious.

Oh, wait. They never believed it was possible.

Mom takes me by the shoulders. "I've been waiting for any excuse to get your father away from this godforsaken state. We want you to visit whenever possible. Or better still, come and live with us. No one is kicking you out of the nest. But please, Lia, don't make me feel guilty for leaving."

I give her an "okay" with a cluck of my tongue.

She chooses to ignore what she would otherwise interpret as disrespect, her desperate plea not a lie.

Dad's face is red from lifting all the bags into the trunk and backseat of their Cadillac. He finally has enough breath to agree with Mom's assessment of me. "We raised her well."

He pulls out his wallet and hands me a stack of bills. "We had this tucked away in the safe. Use it to get off-island if they call an official evacuation. Then use the rest to come home to Florida."

They hug and kiss me goodbye, calling out I love you's after they get situated. As though my parents planned for months, they wave, put the car in drive, and peal out of the parking lot, leaving me standing with a thousand dollars and a dream that may never come true.

Brandon calls from the kitchen, "Three clams and onion," and I get back to work.

9

GREG

"*Moonlight Melody* transcends, no matter your age, race, or creed." Alicia defends the show adamantly.

At her comment, I almost drop the 4'x8' sheet of plywood I'm holding up for Jack to screw over the final window on the Beachy Keen cottage.

"Puh-lease!" I exclaim with a groan. "How many times can they say 'You're moony!' in a single show?" I streamed one episode and wished I had left well enough alone. It's like my brain has a stain of ick from the one viewing of the corny, cheesy show forever.

Behind me, my mom, Jack, Alicia, Gabe, Dan, and Clara, bellow, "No, you're moony!" the response residents of the moon give to each other whenever the word gets uttered.

Near as I can tell, moony means both "hello" and "good-bye," "silly" and "serious," and somehow also "I want you" and "You bastard!"

When they aren't saying stupid catchphrases, they line dance in the town square on a whim or get caught up in murderous love triangles, where sex is always the punishment and the payoff for any crime.

"And why is the leader of a moon colony called President Poseidon? Shouldn't they be living under the sea?"

I defy anyone to explain what the show is supposed to be about.

Colleen answers, "They live in the Sea of Tranquility," like it's obvious.

"Which is a basin on the moon caused by volcanic eruptions eons ago that only looked like oceans to the first astronomers. Apollo 11 landed there in 1969. Remember? The old pictures show moon dust spewing from beneath Neil Armstrong's boots." My short Social Studies session underlines the stupidity of the show's storyline.

"Lighten up, Greg!" Alicia admonishes. "It's a twist on literal definitions."

"A nautical twist!" Gabe imparts to the amusement of everyone but me.

"Please, enough!" I beg. "Can we stop talking about the insipid show and focus on getting out of here?"

They all laugh at me, the keepers of some inside joke that I'll never understand because the show makes no sense, and no one will ever convince me otherwise

But finally, gratefully, they shut up and get back to work.

Jack and I have been on plywood duty for the last six hours. Unlike many residents of Bristlemouth, we didn't have to bee-line it for the hardware store for supplies. Jack boards the rental properties up every off-season, and the lab was built as a backup emergency shelter to the elementary school; the state-of-the-art building isn't going anywhere.

Mom and Clara fill up the cars with suitcases and things they can't bear to live without, and Alicia and Gabe pack up Dan's massive SUV with the motley crew of animals Dan keeps. As the island vet, it's a variety pack of misfits: four dogs, a cat, three ferrets, two lovebirds, an albino python, and six backyard chickens.

Gabe can't help with the heavy plywood because of an old shoulder injury, so he and Alicia picked pet detail. They're probably the only two who drove onto the island. After the evacuation order became official, the crowds headed in the opposite direction. Jack owns eight properties: his own house, six rentals, and the lab, so packing up and leaving entailed more for us.

It's a shame Lia's dream is over. Gino Lawson texted Jack last night, telling us his flight was canceled, nothing coming in or out of Logan in Boston or T.F. Green in Providence until they know precisely how bad the storm will be. It could still be a Category 2 or 3, which the island has endured loads of in the past, but if it hits a Cat 5, yeah, we're screwed.

I've tried calling Lia's cell phone every hour since Gino texted, but she's not answering. She's probably already left the island, heartbroken.

It sucks I won't see her until Thanksgiving break, and that's if I'm lucky. Except for a couple interludes, the best one in the kitchen two nights ago, I barely got to see her all summer, so my plan to woo her back never panned out.

Jack and Mom are bringing me back to school once we leave the island. We'll drive into the storm and stop at my oldest friend Nathan's house in Rhode Island to ride out the worst of it. The head start will get me back just in time for the first class.

Brandon pulls up along the curb in his Mini Cooper as the last screw gets drilled into the plywood. He jogs across the lawn, frantic.

"Lia won't leave! Her parents took a flight out yesterday,

and she refused to go with them. I begged her to come with us. But I'm getting nowhere with her."

Alicia overhears and interjects, "Brandon! You are not staying here one second longer than Gabe and me. We are following you to your cousins' house, and that's final."

Brandon bites his tongue, nodding to indicate he agrees with her demand. He'd no more talk back to his mother than set himself on fire. He pulls me around the back of the cottage, away from attentive ears.

"Greg, will you do it? You know I can't say no to my mother, but Lia needs help. It's like she's consumed with saving the restaurant and can't grasp how dangerous the storm might become. You talk to her. She might listen to you, seeing that you guys have, you know—" He pauses, encouraging me to fill in the blanks.

"Made up?" I'm purposefully obtuse. Unless she told, no one knows him barging in on us in the kitchen wasn't our most embarrassing moment.

He claps me on the back, laughing. "Yeah. Made up." He jogs toward the front yard where Alicia taps her foot impatiently and calls his name and waves goodbye. "Thanks, buddy. Catch you when you get back."

My mother is no less a worry-wort than his. How do I convince her to let me follow them out?

Jack.

I peek around the corner of the house and spy him checking the panels one final time. I only have to wait a few seconds before he comes around back.

He jumps. "Greg! Don't creep up on me like that."

"Shhh!" I admonish, pulling him out of sight from the others. "Listen, I need your help."

I fill him in on Lia, and he looks ready to reject my idea

to use Clara's old car, which they're leaving behind, and meet them within the hour.

"Before you say no, answer this: If this was you, would you leave my mom behind?"

He rolls his eyes heavenward, hands on his hips, stretching his lower back. "Dammit, Greg! Of course not. I wouldn't leave you or her." He sighs and drops his hands before continuing, "Or anyone behind for that matter." He sticks a finger in my face. "You have one hour. If you don't meet us, we're coming back to get you. Lia or no Lia." He pauses, realizing with the clouds thick and dark above our heads that once a person leaves, there's no coming back until Fender, the hurricane, passes.

"Please, convince Lia as fast as possible, and get out of here before it's too late."

"I'll try. What are you going to tell Mom?"

"The truth. That you're a man, a caring one, and that we Bryants' help others in need— especially those we love.

"Now, listen, if getting off-island ceases to be an option, go to the lab. Bring all the bedding, cans of food, and bottles of water you can find." Jack reaches into his pocket and hands me the master keys to all the rental units. The move is futile, and he pockets them once more. With the cottages boarded up, I'll have to access the stocked guest pantries another way. "If you think you have enough water, double the amount. Don't forget: you need two hand-operated can openers, just in case.

"Above all, be safe, be smart, and don't take risks. I love you, Greg." He pulls me in for a hug. After growing up without a dad, it's one of the greatest feelings to have such a stellar fill-in.

"I love you, too. Tell Mom not to be mad."

We laugh.

"Good luck with Lia. If the bridge doesn't overflow, meet us at Nathan's. Otherwise, call the moment you can. You'll have power from the generator, but you won't have cell service once the wind picks up."

We feel the first drops of rain on our foreheads.

With one hand on my shoulder as he passes to join the caravan, Mom honking the horn for us to hurry, Jack wishes me, "Good luck."

"See ya, Jack."

❧

Lia sits on the dock, drenched. Her natural flaxen hair appears dyed brown, pasted to her cheeks and neck. Her pink sweatshirt does nothing to keep her dry as it sags off of one shoulder, dripping water onto her bare legs in jean shorts.

She startles when I sit next to her, engrossed in her pain, tears streaming down her cheeks.

"It's gone." She points to where the bridge still stands, water rising, nearly unusable, the waves crash over it, one after the other, in a steady torrent.

The dock swells beneath us like a carnival ride for toddlers. Though we're protected on one side of the inlet with marshland and the other by manufactured things like the restaurant, parking lot, and street beyond, it won't be long before the bridge and the marsh will disappear. Who knows where the waterline on land will end? Hope has me believing it already reached its peak.

"We have to go, Lia. You're all wet." I stand and reach for her hand. She pulls it away harshly.

"I'm not leaving. Don't you see, Greg? While everything remains, there's still a chance I could get her back."

I don't see, but I'll play along if agreeing will get her

safely indoors. "Sure. But does being soaked to the skin help anything? I don't see any reason why we can't gather supplies and hole up somewhere. Then we'll come up with a plan of attack."

Lia shakes her head and folds her arms around her body. She's not swayed.

"Clara keeps the deep freezer stocked."

If Clara's baked goods can't get a person out of a funk, nothing can.

Lia leaps to stand and beats me to the restaurant's back door. "Are you coming?" she calls over her shoulder. "I've got to grab a few things and lock up."

Whew! My initial plan to reconnect with Lia may be dead in the water, but the universe just placed a new one right in my lap.

I'm up and following her like the moon in the earth's gravitational pull.

10

LIA

Since everything went sideways, I haven't had much of an appetite, making the chocolate chip cookies taste divine. The perfectly blended butter, chocolate, and sugar melt in my mouth before swallowing. It's the perfect cookie ingesting system: bite, melt, savor, swallow, repeat.

One after another goes down the gullet until a baker's dozen rests in my belly.

Neither of us has spoken a word since we left the restaurant.

Greg drove us down streets, white-knuckled, littered with branches, and flooded with massive puddles to Dan and Clara's place to pick up provisions. The wind, growing stronger by the second, threatened to knock the car over if he dared drive over twenty miles an hour.

With all the typical entrances nailed shut, we used the bulkhead, entering a dirt-lined crawlspace that led to a pull-down ladder beneath a hatch in the kitchen. A few old mason jars lined up on a thin wood shelf indicate the space was used as a root cellar at one point. The contents within looked like science experiments from a sick mind.

Dark as night inside, Greg used his headlamp to light our way; the electricity shut down ten minutes earlier. We heard the motorized sounds of generators turning on during rare breaks in the screeching wind.

I packed anything I could get my hands on in the kitchen, including the promised contents of the deep freeze, while Greg stripped the beds of linens and pillows.

The final leg of the drive turns out to be scarier than the first. The downed branches of earlier are replaced now by entire trees. The only street still accessible closed the moment we pulled into the lab's parking lot when a utility pole fell across the whole span of the lane. We're here for good—or until help arrives back on the island.

Greg parks inches from the front door, and we carry everything inside. It takes the two of us to hold the door closed enough for him to lock us in.

The dwelling is solid with thick glass and cement walls. Our ears finally get a break from the deafening wind, rain, and shattering trees as we stand in the reception area.

"You okay?" he asks, soaked top to toe from walking the two-foot span between the car and building.

"Maybe. Probably. You?"

"Now that the drive is over, sure."

"I don't need any more of these." I hand over the box of cookies, and he tucks it under his arm.

"Come on. We'll put our stuff in the break room, and I'll give you a tour."

The bright overhead lighting, courtesy of the massive generator, gives a sense of normalcy and removes some of the fear and gloom of the harrowing drive.

As Greg referred to it, the break room consists of a microwave, hotplate, futon couch, and an overturned crate for a table. Efficiency never looked so welcome. The room is dry, with an attached bathroom to the right. Chills from being wet so long have my body shivering and in need of a quick warm-up.

"Mind if I shower first?"

"Not at all. We have plenty of time for you to look around."

"Thanks." I pull my message bag from the pile of goods and close the bathroom door behind me.

Greg

I'm blowing this!

I should've asked Lia if she wanted company. Then again, she might think I'm taking advantage. On the other hand, we'll only be stranded for a short time. The evacuation is a sure-fire way to keep us from getting caught, as is our tendency.

Of course, once the bridge opens up, I'll be heading back to school, the recent turn of events already likely to make me late.

But—

I've run out of hands and excuses and choose to stop overthinking. I may have missed my window of opportunity this time, but I'll prepare better for the next.

I peel off my wet layers and pull on dry shorts and a sweatshirt. Warmer already, I unpack our provisions, line up the canned goods to keep track, and put the perishables in the mini fridge. We have more than enough food, but the clothing might become an issue. Jack never planned for a seasonal boarder living in the lab, so most of my stuff is still at the house.

I shrug. Naked works for me. Maybe Lia feels the same.

Just as I'm about to knock on the bathroom door to ask if she needs anything, like company, she screams bloody-blue murder.

"Greg! Someone's looking in the window!"

No time for questions, I'm out the door. Only one narrow alley outside allows access past the bathroom, and even then they'd need a ladder to see inside. What level of derelict is willing to risk their lives in a hurricane to get a peek at a young woman? It doesn't matter; I'll catch them.

I run through the hallways, toward the back of the building, knowing whoever this is will hit the chainlink fence that prevents pedestrians from absently walking into the main thoroughfare.

He'll have to double back or climb over the wall, grown thick with ivy. As a scholarship track and field student with a high jump of seven and a half feet, it's unlikely the criminal will be anywhere near as capable as me.

Covered from head to toe in black sweats, the guy runs like a tree sloth after an enormous lunch. I could catch him in my sleep.

Five feet from the fence, I grab a fistful of his sweatshirt and spin him around before shoving him against the wall with my forearm across his chest beneath his quivering chin.

"Let me go!" Steve screams like a girl.

It's rare to discover traces of my deceased father's traits inside me. Sure, I have some of his physical characteristics, but by all accounts Mason was a badass with a bad attitude. Me? I like to think I could hold my own in a fistfight, but my life hasn't made that level of aggression necessary.

My fist flies back involuntarily, ready to strike him square on the jaw. At the last second, I drop it and loosen my hold on the guy in deference to Jack and his more peaceful approach to life. Steve will get what's coming to him. I'll make sure of it.

"You're going to jail!" I yell into his ugly, blubbering asshole face.

The wind and rain have leaves and scraps of paper sticking to our skin and clothes. The cacophonous noise is reminiscent of a locomotive barreling down the rails as it races through the alleyway.

Swiping at tears, he talks tough while putting distance between us. "You've got nothing on me! I'm only here to get the keys to the restaurant anyway. How was I to know when I walked by Lia would be showing off?"

"She's on the second floor, idiot! You left the ladder leaning against the windowsill. We're telling Chief Scott the second he gets back about this and how you attacked her at the ballgame and again at the restaurant. We'll see how many people want to visit the restaurant once they know what a scumbag you are!"

"Ooh! I'm telling!" Steve taunts me before tripping over a wayward plastic swan-shaped float from a backyard pool. He lands with a satisfying thud, knocking his head on the exterior wall, leaving a smear of blood.

His hand shoots up to the wound, and he shows me the damage. "You got nothing on me. Your word against mine. But it looks like I've got proof right here." His dark beady eyes squint. "There I was, Chief Scott, minding my own business, and this little boy sucker punches me for a box of Little Debbie snack cakes."

The tale is ludicrous. No one in Bristlemouth eats Little Debbie with Clara around.

Still, the asshole is right. Stories are stories without evidence to back them up, and blood is more potent than words, which leaves only one thing left to say. "The next time

I see you within a hundred feet of Lia, I'm going to kick your ass."

He smirks and rises to stand.

I tense my body, ready to swing for real this time, and he runs away—faster now, like how that same sloth would show up hungry for his meal after a long nap.

❧

Lia

Greg returns, dripping in another outfit saturated with water. He sits quietly beside me on the edge of the futon where I've been hiding under every scrap of bedding since he ran out.

"That was Steve," he says. "You probably already guessed. Can I get you anything?"

I shake my head and lunge onto his lap. He spends the next twenty minutes soothing me, saying all the right things to assure me I'm safe.

"He won't come near you with me or any of my uncles close by."

"Yeah, but he still gets the restaurant."

The truth shocks the same as seeing a pair of eyes in a once-empty window.

"It's not fair, Lia. I wish there were something we could do, but you're right."

Hearing Greg agree with me releases another torrent of tears, and I cry until I'm drained, wetting our clothes further.

"You'd better dry off. I rinsed and jumped out of the shower faster than—" I pause mid-sentence, allowing the sound of the storm to fill the space, and finish, "a Category 5 gale, so there should be plenty hot water left."

Greg kisses me sweetly on top of the head before gathering his things and heading for the bathroom.

Within minutes, steam follows him out the bathroom door, where he stands dressed in shorts and a T-shirt. At the rate we're going, we'll be naked as babies before help arrives.

I blush as the thought brings forward the memory of our first time together. Greg did everything perfectly right; his willingness to please me was more of an aphrodisiac than I would have thought possible. Candles, rose petals, fresh sheets, and soft music made the cottage a cozy, safe cocoon in which to lose our virginity.

We'd planned it almost from the first night we met. At first, in our minds, but then a shared desire. Neither of us could picture such a momentous occasion with anyone else, so knowing Greg would soon head for a college many miles away meant waiting was out of the question.

Greg had insisted, "You just have to show up. I'll do everything else." We laughed hysterically at his wording as I offered, "I can probably do something."

As expected, it was painful that first time. But after a brief pause and some pretty experienced moves for an inexperienced guy, the second time was magical and so swoony.

That was until his mother showed up.

We sat up in shock, and I thought for sure Colleen was going to drop dead in front of us. Everything stopped, and just as quickly, it began moving super fast.

Greg covered us in the cotton sheets. Colleen started freaking out, screaming, "What are those?" pointing at a box of condoms before running to the bathroom to throw up.

I giggle about the traumatic moment under the blankets now as I watch Greg heat us canned ravioli for dinner on the hotplate.

"Laughter's a good sign," he says without turning around. "What's so funny?"

As I remember the look of shock on Greg and Colleen's faces, the tension I've been holding onto these last few days releases, and my giggle turns into peels of bellyaching laughter.

"Your face!" I shriek, bent over my lap, trying to calm the hysteria.

He turns, wearing an expression similar to that night, and I'm howling more than before.

"No. No. No." I hold up a finger to stop him as he saunters toward the bed like a panther. "Not how you look right now. That first ni-ni-night!"

He knows which night I'm referring to when his shocked look turns dark with lust.

Tears stream down my cheeks, and I give in, allowing the humor to roll me onto my back, knees tucked in tight to my abdomen. "I-I-I'm suh-orry! I can't stop laughing!"

Greg pushes angles his body over mine. "I'll stop you if you'd like," he offers, taking my face in his warm hands and cleaning the tears from my cheeks with his thumbs. He catches my next laugh in his mouth and replaces it with his tongue.

He wasn't kidding; all laughter ceases.

11

GREG

Lia quiets instantly, letting me position myself between her legs so we can be as close as possible while we kiss and enjoy the friction. The masculine scented shampoo and soap I've used all summer long smell way better in her hair and on her skin than they ever have on mine. Making a mental note to order it by the case, to never forget this moment, I let thinking go and just feel her kiss, her touch, her thighs clutching my hips.

Lia's hands grip my hair, left longer because she told me it was her preference. Her rich, throaty moans encourage us to explore.

When my hands leave her face to sneak under her shirt, Lia shifts, and I remove it entirely. Braless beneath, her breasts are more glorious than I recall, and I'm lost in my desire to consume her. She removes my shirt then raises the stakes by pulling my shorts down with my boxers, and now I'm the one most exposed.

With a nod to her positive attitude, I have her shorts off, and as with her top, find her lovely body naked beneath.

No longer breathless from my need, I'm thirsting to experience Lia.

Her hands clutch tighter, pulling my hair by the roots, the pain a pleasure adding to the sensations as she brings my face between her legs where we both want it. She guides me with a nuanced roll of her hips, and I feast for what feels like seconds, but by her third climax, she's pushing me away, begging for mercy.

"Please, stop for a second." She sits up on the edge of the futon, pushing me off the bed, forcing me to stand. Her exhalation long, Lia wipes her brow with the back of her wrist. "How can anything feel that good?" Her torso flushes pink, and male pride swells my ego.

I shrug, pretending I knew all along she'd enjoy my efforts when I'm relieved I mastered the lesson her body instructed.

Lia kneels on the floor before me with a saucy look and zero warning and returns the oral favor.

"Whoa!" I can't help from exclaiming, not having expected reciprocity. That she's agreed to be naked with me already feels like the ultimate gift.

Just as Lia discovered, I find the sensations are too much and ask her to stop. "I can't, Lia. I can't hold back."

Too polite to speak with her mouth full, Lia teases with her tongue a little more, like she knows my body better than me. A heartbeat in time passes, then she eases up before my orgasm rockets through me.

Gratitude hardly begins to describe how I feel at this moment. Because I can't explain it, I show her instead. Pulling her to me, so we're both standing, bodies pressed tightly once more, I kiss her deeper than ever. Our flavors blend into a timeless elixir of lust, passion, and love.

"Where'd you learn to do that?" I ask and instantly regret the question. "Forget it. I don't want to know."

She explains anyway as I lay her gently down and join her after rearranging the bedding so we can comfortably rest up for the next round.

"You know my friend Tanya? The slim, birdlike brunette who goes from sweet and shy to obnoxious and outspoken if you give her a beer? Kind of like a Gremlin getting food after midnight only prettier?"

I nod, her description so spot on.

"She showed me."

"Um. What?"

"She showed *everyone* in tenth grade at a bonfire. Someone had to give her a drink, and somehow she got her hands on a banana, and… Well, you can fill in the rest."

"And that's it?"

Lia struggles to push away and sit up. Her brow furrows as she tucks a blanket across her chest. "Oh. I'm sorry. Not good enough for you?"

"No! Don't go anywhere! Words can hardly describe your talent, but I'll try: Awesome. Amazing. Incredible." I recall as many positive adjectives as possible and share them to convince her to stay. "Phenomenal. Remarkable. Bewildering. Beguiling."

Lia lets me continue until I'm stuck on a litany of B-words. "Bewitching. Brilliant. Beauteous."

"All right. That will be enough." She snuggles in close, her head resting on my shoulder. Hiding a yawn in her fist, she turns the tables on me. "Where did you learn, big college boy."

"Big college man," I correct her and joke. "Same place."

She whips up, balancing her weight with her hand on my chest, shock on her face. "Tanya? She's my best friend."

"Not like that, silly. From my friends. Guy talk. No props or visual aids, just ribald stuff. But, if you distill what they say, you can usually find the truth somewhere within."

"So-o-o," she draws out the word, "have you ever done that with anyone but me?"

Honesty is the hardest part of any relationship, at least, that's what Jack tells me. He says with absolute honesty, you can create your version of the perfect relationship, and without it, you'll destroy any bond, no matter how strong or permanent you might believe it to be.

"No. Except for kissing, you've been first and last for everything. You?"

"Same. We must be naturals because that was goo-oo-ood!" She gives her last word three syllables, underlining just how good.

"How is that possible? You're beautiful."

"Thanks." She kisses my knuckles and plays with my fingers. The distraction makes it easier for us to open up. "It's not that simple, is it? I never said guys don't try. I am pretty cute." Her snort-laugh is adorable, but she covers her face, laughing. "Sorry! I'm always doing that."

"I've noticed. Don't apologize. You're adorable." I kiss the tip of her nose and ask her to continue.

"I haven't met anyone like you, Greg. You know? Your mom may have ruined things for us too soon, but you already made your mark and set the bar high."

"You're reading my mind right now. I couldn't have said it better."

We roll over to face each other, heads resting on fluffy pillows, our hands entwined. "I date girls. We go to parties, maybe meet in the cafeteria for lunch or dinner, take in a movie on a Saturday night. But I don't find the spark or level of comfort we share. That's part of why you're so incredible,

Lia—your ability to drive me wild physically but also for making me feel welcome and accepted and home."

She presses her body the length of mine, her skin hot against me. "You see me, Greg. That's your superpower." She kisses me deeply, and instantly we're thick in the middle of experimenting, exploring, and pleasing each other.

As I slide inside Lia's body, uniting us completely, my need for her has less to do with the physical. Something more vital stirs within, and I know I'll love this woman forever.

The hurricane blows harder after the eye of the storm passed overhead while we slept, ensconced in our private world. We'll have to pack up once the wind slows to prepare for the islanders' return to rebuild. Lia will also have to hand the restaurant key over to Steve, a prospect neither of us is looking forward to.

"Thanks for offering, Greg, but I need to hand it over myself." Lia sits on the futon, now raised now into a couch position, eating ravioli, helping me polish off four cans after our other appetites vetoed our desire to play some more.

"I'll be right next to you. He's not going to try a damn thing." I take her free hand and kiss her palm. "Are you okay?"

She shakes her head and takes another bite. "No. I'm freaking out a little. Without the restaurant as a mooring, I'm lost." She sits back, shoulders slumped, and hands me her empty bowl. Stacking it with mine, I take it to the sink and give the items a rinse before grabbing a box of Lia's favorite Clara-made cookies.

She bites into the Snickerdoodle, closing her eyes to relish the flavor. "So good," she determines. "What isn't good is that I'm going to be living in a carport at my parents' place in Florida. How lame am I? My life was planned for me, and I was on board. 'Hand me a business, and I'll do you proud.' I've always said that to my dad. And here we are. My parents are broke. My mother vows to never come back to this 'god-forsaken place,' and that weasel is the one who wins. Life is so unfair!"

It's hard to find the right words, but I can't let her think I don't care. "Did you ever have a second dream? A backup plan? Maybe something you wanted to explore as a hobby or in an alternative universe?"

Though technically a snort, the sound she makes isn't cute but jaded. "Maybe I could live with Gino Lawson on the moon."

"Anywhere but there, please," I beg. "Come on. I know you dreamed of something beyond the restaurant."

Instead of answering, Lia grabs her messenger bag, pulls out a thick notebook, and hands it to me. "Look at this."

Inside I find indecipherable notations, phone numbers, addresses, and loads of photos. "What's this?"

"My diary, I guess you could say. Ever since I was little,I've been fascinated with faraway places. Whenever anyone new visited The Clam Digger, I'd sit and listen, enraptured with their stories. It didn't matter whether they came from somewhere as close as Boston or as far away as the Philippines. The minor details of their lives were somehow similar to my experience and yet exotic because they happened somewhere else." She reaches for the book and points to a picture toward the back.

"See that?"

Waves of green ether fill the background, while in the foreground, a woman stands with her back to the viewfinder, topless in a partially frozen lake. Whoever took the picture was a true professional based on the evocative nature of the print. It's stunning.

"That's incredibly artistic."

She nods in agreement. "If things were different, I'd travel the world. Ask people basic questions about their day-to-day lives, and match them with photos of what they see most." She flips through the pages and finds another incredible picture, though less colorful and dramatic.

A drab and primitive door made of thick planks of wood weighs heavy on rusty hinges, a handmade, brilliant green and red holly wreath displayed on its center. The contrast catches the eye, with nothing in the shot being extraordinary. Like the first print, it tells a story that words could never describe.

"I get it!" I'm as excited about the prospect as she should be. "You should do this!"

She rejects the idea as she takes the book away. "It's a pipe dream. No money equals no education, which equals Lia looking for a job in a restaurant someone else owns in sunny, buggy Florida."

"Don't be a quitter, Lia, especially before you've begun. I've met plenty of students whose parents can't pay for college. I'm on a scholarship, but you can find grants, loans, and other ways to make it work. I'm sure your parents can kick in something. You're willing to work, and my mom is a seasoned expert in filling out college applications and following the money trail. We'll talk to her when she gets back."

Lia turns pale. "Your mom hates me."

I laugh out loud, her belief preposterous. "My mother hates no one. She really likes you, Lia."

"Did you see her face when she caught me having sex with her boy?"

"She was shocked. Weren't you?"

"Understatement."

"And it was the same for her. She's over it, believe me. It's worth a shot, don't you think?"

She hands over the notebook and a pen before curling up in a blanket and tucking a pillow under her head. "Wake me when you come back to earth," my favorite cynic tells me before falling back to sleep.

Her dreams are in my hands now and, as she snoozes, I scan the pages and reach out to those who might be able to help.

12

LIA

Once the wind dies down to a less life-threatening level, I can't take the seclusion a second longer. Not that staying in Greg's little hideaway forever wouldn't be preferred, but I have to face this awful day before it eats me up from within.

My fingers shake as I fold my wet clothes and pack them with the precision that my departure from the restaurant lacked. Part of me is desperate to see the place one last time before handing over the key, and another wishes to bypass the area and head straight to Logan so I can fly to the carport that awaits. How's that for scared? I'd rather live in a semi-enclosed, surely lizard-riddled space than face Steve.

"You ready?" Greg stands beside me, one hand wrapped around my waist, the other reaching for my bag. He balances all our belongings and additional provisions like a Sherpa, leaving me only my journal to carry. "I made some notes in there. I hope you don't mind."

"Of course not," I whisper, biting down on my inner cheek to stop the tears from starting, knowing Greg's kindness will cause them to fall easier than Steve's ugliness.

Memories of his horrible face flash through my mind as he watched me in the bathroom window, like a moss-ridden concrete gargoyle from *Dante's Inferno*.

Goose-over-your-grave shivers run down my spine, and I need to flee. "Let's go."

Greg follows me down the stark white halls of the laboratory building, and I remember we never went on the tour Greg promised. A thin smile breaks through the gloom, recognizing what we shared was much better than that. Plus, perhaps it will give me an excuse to come back and visit him sometime.

The truth of the situation punches me in my already sensitive gut space as I fold into the passenger seat of Clara's beater-box car: Greg and I are parting today. The water will recede, the bridge will open so the residents can return, and Greg will leave for South Carolina. It doesn't matter if I'm in Massachusetts or Florida—he won't be there.

And knowing this, my tears release. I make no noise, letting them flow as Greg drives beside me, so focused on getting us safely to our destination that he's unaware. Debris of all sorts litters the streets. Trees, plastic kiddie pools, patio umbrellas, and anything that was not battened down make for hazardous driving conditions. Greg hunches like an old man over the wheel, making sharp twitchy movements to avoid the detritus, a tough maneuverability test, no cones necessary.

Usually a five-minute drive on a clear day, it takes us thirty minutes to turn onto A Street where The Clam Digger was built many moons ago.

"A restaurant built on the prettiest inlet shore, offering good food at a great price." My dad insisted employees open with that line whenever speaking to a person unfamiliar with the establishment.

Greg parks the car in the middle of the street. Parking

meters and laws hold no weight when you're stranded and alone.

Almost alone. Steve the Perv waits a few feet away, his face a pale mask of shock and awe. Surely it's the same expression Greg and I wear as well.

"Greg? Where are we?" I foolishly ask. I played hopscotch in the corner of this parking lot and hide-n-seek in the reeds surrounding it. A funny, outgoing Brit visiting with his parents, Kenny Clifton, gave me my first kiss under the Japanese maple by the decorative fountain and miniature replica of Bristlemouth Bridge, now just a heap of debris.

Greg checks the GPS on his phone, absurd as service hasn't resumed yet. "This is it, Lia."

"It's gone. Everything." My hand, held aloft like a spokesmodel, hits the passenger side window. The smack of my fingertips on the glass makes it all real.

The parking lot is a trash receptacle for seaweed. Faded red-leather upholstered booths, broken and torn, lay on top like massive cooked lobsters. Shattered plates, scattered utensils, everything you'd expect to find inside a restaurant now rests outside.

What we can't wrap our heads around is the restaurant itself. Nothing stands. Not a dock piling, wall stud, or roofing shingle exists, all swept out to sea.

Slowly, we unbuckle our seatbelts and crawl out of the vehicle. With the slamming of the car doors, Steve awakes from his stupor and flies at me in a rage.

"Where is it?" Stupidity spreads in the best of times, so the remark makes sense; we're all in shock.

"Gone!" I shriek without meaning to, louder than the storm's harshest tone. "Don't you see? Everything my family worked for, everything I stood to gain, everything you tried to steal, it's all gone."

Greg stands between us, ready to fight.

I'm not sure which of us he'll need to defend. Holding the restaurant key between my index and middle finger, I'm prepared to shove it in Steve's eye.

"Stand back." Greg's warning is enough to make Steve comply, then he looks at me and asks the question most on his mind lately, "You okay?"

I can't speak for a moment. It's more than I can bear. The restaurant is gone, not broken, not in need of repair, just gone. My parents are gone. Greg leaves today. And my future floats in limbo. The fleeting nature of every moment hits me like an awakening.

So I laugh. It's shocking, overwhelming, and absurd, and I love it!

Both men stare like I've lost my mind. Greg tries to calm what he perceives as hysteria while Steve repeatedly demands, "Give me the key."

I love Greg, and I kiss him to prove how much. "I'm okay," I insist.

He searches my face for the truth, finds it, and smiles before kissing me back.

The warmth of his embrace is too comforting to ignore, so I remain snuggled deep as I turn to Steve and toss the key high in the air. He catches it, a winner's grin on his face.

"Where do you think you're going to stick that, idiot?" I ask, emboldened with Greg as my fierce protector.

Steve's sexual sneer is no surprise, and he leers at me before Greg punches him square in the jaw, felling him with one strike.

"Your gonna pay for that," Steve threatens, spitting blood as he struggles to get up and avoid Greg's strike zone. Swiping at his lip with his forearm, Steve threatens me. "I can't wait to see your face after I rebuild and you show up groveling for a job."

"I've paid more than my fair share by losing my inheritance."

This day I thought would be so terrible gets brighter by the moment. Instead of heartbreak over the loss of the restaurant, I feel a weight lifting off my shoulders. It flies high above us before crashing back to earth to land on top of Steve.

Let him carry it!

"Hey, Steve. Did you read that contract all the way through? You know, all the little details the town put in that had nothing to do with my dad, your father, or the restaurant itself."

"So what?" With his cocky attitude back, Steve holds the steel key high in the air. "It's mine. Coulda been yours, too, if you just said yes to my proposal."

Fighting back the need to vomit at his last words, I take pleasure in sharing the facts. "Actually, it's not. It's not mine, and it's not yours. If you go to page three, article four, you'll find a paragraph which stipulates, 'Should the edifice itself be irreparable for any reason, including, but not limited to, acts of God, process of condemnation by federal, state, or local authorities, arson, or other criminal intent, decisions for the use of said six-acre parcel of land returns to its rightful owner, the town of Bristlemouth Bay.'" I quote it verbatim after memorizing every word of the document when I wished to save the business.

Greg and Steve stare at me agog.

"Bullshit!" Steve exclaims.

I turn on my heel and march back to the car without a word. From inside the front pocket of my bag, I pull out the agreements. Half of the papers are the signed deal between my great grandfather and the original owner of The Clam Digger, Douglas Jeffries, and his father-in-law, Jonas Falk, the mayor of Bristlemouth Bay way back. From day one, the deal was that the Jeffries owned the building, the town, the land, period.

The second agreement is the contract between Steve's parents and mine, the one he should have read as it also decrees his future within.

As I make my way back to the car, I flip through both documents to the correct page in each that spells out what Bristlemouth Bay has been waiting for in plain English. For years, the powers have wanted this space to convert the acreage and ocean inlet to a wind turbine farm, and now they have it.

My relatives stayed one step ahead by remaining in the good graces of the town and its citizens and were always able to rebuild. The restaurant lost a wall here and there, and, of course, the dock the year of Steve's parents' loan, but it never disappeared. Because of the stringent stipulation, even if I had somehow been able to retain ownership from all my hard work and careful planning, I too would have lost The Clam Digger. What a hoot!

"You can keep these," I offer sweetly, handing the stack of papers over to Steve. "Copies. The original is filed at the town hall. Talk to the selectman about the particulars if you're still at a loss."

Steve scans the papers and lets the dying wind take them from his hands, one by one, as reality sinks in.

"Buh-bye, Steve," I say to his dumbstruck face. Greg and I leave him amid the litter and walk back to the car.

"Where do you think he'll end up?" Greg asks, getting the door for me.

"Back to mommy and daddy first, jail eventually."

"Appropriate," Greg quips.

He turns on the car and exclaims, "Lia, look!" He points toward the bridge. Dozens of vehicles idle and wait their turn to head over the pass and back home.

"Yay." My response lacks enthusiasm.

"It's going to work out, Lia. Promise."

I smile because, for him, the statement is true. As for me? I don't know a thing.

13

GREG

If staying were an option. I'd unpack our bags and move Lia into the break room of the lab, where we could maintain the splendor of the fantasy days we lived locked up, safe from the elements.

But my mom would kill me, and she's freaking out.

"Mom! I'm already late for everything, including my classes. All my professors approved the makeup work, so one more day won't make a difference. I'll worry about it after Jack drops me off."

She opens her mouth to argue, and Jack cuts in.

"He's a man, Colleen. Do we need to have this talk again so soon?" Jack's loving smile buffers the words my mother hates to hear.

She'd have me swaddled in a blue blanket with a pacifier stuck in my mouth if she could get away with it.

Throwing up her hands, she accedes. "Fine. You're right. We could use an extra pair of hands with Gabe back to work at the fire station. I'll work with Lia. Clara and Alicia, do you want to help?" The ladies nod, happy to avoid the heavy lifting.

Jack, Dan, and I gather the tools necessary to set things back to rights then hop into Dan's SUV to make the rounds.

The animals in the back create a stir, so we head to Dan's house first. Luckily everything seems intact, including the chicken coop. He unpacks the animals while Jack and I remove the plywood and check inside the house for water damage. It's like the day of the evacuation, only backward.

The time flies after we check every cottage and then go food shopping. We don't find much fresh food, so we stock up on frozen stuff.

When we arrive back at the house, Lia meets me outside the front door and kisses me deeply after saying "hello" to Jack and Dan as they pass.

"How am I going to go a full day without seeing you? Let alone months or years?"

"Not years" is the only promise I can make. "Let's talk."

We walk over to a macramé swing that somehow survived the storm. After I untwist its length, Lia sits on my lap, and I use my feet to move us gently back and forth, then side to side. We watch Jack and Dan fire up the grill to cook the frozen hamburgers and corn on the cob.

"This is why I wanted to stay the extra night—so that we could figure stuff out. Most importantly, how was today? Did my mother behave?"

She nods. "I'm overwhelmed, but you were right: Colleen is a pro at this stuff." Then goes on to explain how they spent the day printing applications for colleges with bachelor's in arts degree programs, loans, grants, and scholarships.

Lia rests her head on my chest and sighs. "It all comes back to grades and money. My grades were good, mostly B's, an A here and there, and I was no stranger to a C, but the money." She shakes her head slowly, side to side, like a massage, and my overused pec muscles relax. "It's a lot."

"Don't give up."

She angles her head and kisses me, promising, "I won't. So what else is on your mind?"

I'd rather have a lobotomy than share this with her, but as it pertains to nobody else, and I have no choice. "I don't want this to end, but I also can't expect you to wait. You need to feel free to date other guys.

"I want you to know I kick myself all the time for not finding you the first time I came home the first year. If I apologized then, who knows where our relationship would be now?"

"Oh, I don't know, Greg. I could have done the same. Maybe not the apology part, but I certainly could have acted normal instead of pretending like you didn't exist, even when you were standing next to me." She turns and curls herself up in a ball on her side. I have to cradle her bum in both hands to stop her from falling—a good deal by anyone's estimation. "Can't we chalk all that up to our age and start fresh?"

"Except our fresh start begins with me leaving."

Her eyes widen in alarm. "You're coming back, though, right?"

"Of course. But will you be here?"

"Oh." Her brow furrows, and then she smiles. "Yes! Colleen said I could stay as long as I like. No carport for me! I'll have the Beachy Keen to myself once the rental season ends." Her fingers trace the design on my shirt and an idea dawns. "Maybe we can finish what we started in that bedroom all those years ago when you come home and visit in October."

"It's a deal," is all I can say when her hand sneaks under my shirt, and she follows the thin line of hair on my abdomen up to my belly button before splaying her hand wide and slowly heading back down. No doubt, this woman owns me already.

Still, there's a future at stake here—two of them, so I wrap her fingers in mine and sit up straighter. "Let's wait until the crowd disperses. We'll head over to the cottage tonight and get a head start on your plan."

With a cheeky grin and a kiss, she agrees.

Jack, Colleen, Dan, Clara, and Alicia make a lot of noise as they nurse drinks on the deck and cook.

Ruefully, I break the kiss and clear my throat before returning to the main topic. "So, you can date. I can date."

"You said that," Lia tells me. "Are you trying to tell me have somebody in South Carolina waiting?" Her muscles tense, ready to leap from my lap, and I hold on tight.

"No. I don't want to date anyone else, and I don't want you to date, either. I'm just trying to be reasonable. We're not ready to marry or settle down, and making you sit around and wait would be unfair. Everything is crazy and in flux. I'm there, and you're here—or somewhere. Working on my thesis takes up so much of my time and energy, and—"

"Shut up, Greg."

My head rocks back, and my feet grow still. We sit in the swing without swaying, her smile all that reassures.

"You're always asking, 'Are you okay?' and the answer is yes: It's all okay. I'm on your side, Greg. We have no idea who we'll be down the road, but, honestly? I don't see me on any path you aren't trodding down as well. Maybe we'll stay lovers, and maybe we'll revert to friends. Let's just promise not to become enemies, and the rest can take care of itself."

"It's not that simple, Lia."

"Sure it is. We can make it anything we want. This relationship is ours."

"Hm. I hadn't considered that angle."

"You're not the only one with a brain. Now, kiss me like you never want to leave so I have something to sustain me through dinner."

I start to do just that when her hand pushes me away.

"Why is there a limousine parked outside your house, Greg?"

I shake my head. "I dunno. Should we go see?"

We hold hands on our way to the front and watch as the limo driver steps out and opens the back door. Tanya, Melissa, and Brandon flood out.

"Hey, guys!" Lia drops my hand and darts to her posse, hugging each one in turn. Brandon wears a suit, and the ladies donned airy sundresses for the occasion. Lia looks down at her typical outfit—shorts and a slouchy T-shirt—and readjusts the top, having slipped off her shoulder. "What are you doing here? Did somebody elope?"

Nobody answers; they just step to the side to let a fourth passenger out.

Colleen, Clara, and Alicia gasp from behind us.

Lia shrieks, her hands covering her mouth as she jumps for joy. "It's you!" she repeatedly says until Gino Lawson takes her hand in his and kisses the back of it.

My mother and aunts sigh like they just watched a newborn deer struggle to its feet.

Once he's through playing the part of gallant knight, Gino stands and gestures to the crowd surrounding them. "Your friends let me know you needed help, and President Poseidon never lets a Moonflower wilt."

Everyone laughs but me.

Jack claps me on the back and explains, "Female moon residents are called Moonflowers and the males Moonfaunas."

"That makes no sense," I argue.

"Greg's being moony," Alicia accuses, and everyone agrees by chanting, "Moony, moony, moony," like a bunch of moon bats.

Before I consider murdering them all, I remember what a help everyone has been, including Gino.

When Lia fell asleep in the lab, after permitting me to look through her journal, I made a list of every person inside with whom she'd been in touch within the past year. I prepared a written appeal, and once cell service became available, flooded the phone lines. With the help of family, we spoke or texted with every person on the list—and they all responded immediately with an enthusiastic and loving "yes" to helping Lia.

She thought they only touched her life, but she touched theirs as well.

Money offers began to flood in until Jack got the call from Gino.

"Give it all back," Gino told him. "They can give to someone in actual need. I've got her covered."

When Jack ran Gino's genome years ago, they found out Gino had a half-sister, but she died when she started college. Gino never met Teresa, but he finally met his biological father and stepmother, two hardworking teachers in Detroit.

To honor Teresa, Gino started a scholarship fund for college-bound females. Five women were recipients every year and received a free ride, books, housing, and food included to the four-year college of their choice.

This year's scholarships were already awarded, but Gino approved Lia as next year's first winner. The timing could not have been more perfect as it will take her that long to fill out the forms, wait for approvals, and prepare to move.

But she doesn't know any of this yet.

Gino gives me the floor, and I fill her in. Her hands

tremble as I hold them in mine and hit on all the salient points, finishing with, “Congratulations, Lia! You’re the winner of the Teresa Modestino award.”

With tears of joy and admiration brimming in her eyes, she asks, “Did you do all this, Greg?”

“Everyone helped. From all your friends in your journal, right down to Mr. Lawson. I—we all love you, Lia.”

“That’s the first time you’ve told me that.” Her eyes grow misty before she smacks my shoulder. “And that was my idea you stole!”

I smile sheepishly. “You had a solid plan. I just implemented it.”

“Tell me you love me again,” she demands, and I comply.

“I love you.”

“I love you, Greg!” She plants a kiss on my lips to cheers and applause.

“Let’s Moondance!” Gino calls out, and everyone who watches the show knows what to do—samba, from the looks of it.

Brandon pulls Tanya into his arms. Jack holds tightly to Colleen, and Clara snuggles close to Dan.

The limo driver snags Melissa as she looks around, afraid she’s the only lady without a full dance card. The pair are well-matched in height and obviously have interest in each other.

It appears the only one without a partner is Alicia until Gino takes her by the hand, spins her like a music box ballerina, and lands her against him perfectly posed. “Shall we, my Moonflower extraordinaire?”

No one can deny the man’s showy appeal.

Alicia blushes like a schoolgirl and breathlessly answers, “Yes, Mr. President.”

The lot of them begin to sway.

"Wasn't this your dream—to dance with Poseidon?" I ask Lia. We're the only two not moving. "Should you ask to cut in?"

Lia shakes her pretty head, and her hair glows in the dimming sunshine. "My old dream lies at the bottom of the Atlantic, but my new one is right here, in your arms. Whatever happens in the next few years, wherever we go, together or apart, I'll always come back to this." She shrugs, reminding me how simple life can be if you embrace the flow of its resolute direction. "You're where I belong."

"I couldn't agree more," I confess and twirl her toward the patch of lawn, now dance floor, better than any Moon-fauna—including their president.

The End

THANK YOU READERS

Thank you for reading "A Nautical Twist," Book 4 Bryant Brothers Novella Series. It would mean the world if you took a moment to post a review wherever you purchased the book and let others know what you think. Please visit kathleenpendoley.com, Instagram, Facebook, or Pinterest for information on new releases, blog posts, and more.

Kathleen Pendoley
AUTHOR

ACKNOWLEDGMENTS

Writing a book is never a solitary venture. As such, I'd like to recognize the following people for giving me their time, input, and support; you're priceless!

Thank you to:

Jamie Ross for this beautiful cover and being an all-around inspiration.

Stephanie Blackman, for your expert editing.

Mike Sicilia for adding depth and detail to the plot.

Katheryne Doherty for assuring your Aunt that sex hasn't changed.

Mary and John Kenzierski at www.innatellisriver.com for selling my books in your shop.

My Facebook followers, for brightening my day with your interactions.

And finally, but never last, my husband Paul for keeping the faith when I run out.

ALSO BY KATHLEEN PENDOLEY

Bryant Brothers Novella Series

Beachy Keen - Book 1

The Cake Maker's Dog - Book 2

Glitter and Grief - Book 3

Novels

Trail of the Heart

Made in the USA
Middletown, DE
29 August 2022